MASTER OF FORTUNE

SPECIAL EDITION

SIENNA SNOW

GODS OF VEGAS

BOOK 6

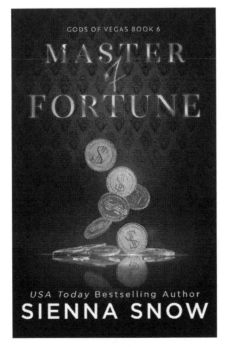

Special Edition

MASTER OF FORTUNE

MASTER OF FORTUNE

SIENNA SNOW

Copyright Page

Cover Design: Steamy Designs

Editor: Jennifer Haymore

www.siennasnow.com

ISBN - eBook - 978-1-948756-38-9

ISBN – Special Edition Cover - Paperback - 979-8-88535-001-3

1

SIMON

"IF YOU HURT HER, THE WAR YOU'LL FACE IS SOMETHING YOU'LL never recover from."

I gave no reaction to Tyler Mykos's threat, only staring into his black eyes. Though, the impulse to reach across the table and punch him in the face sat heavy in the back of my mind.

The fucker thought he held the cards when I was the one who could make or break this whole deal.

A deal worth over a billion fucking dollars.

A deal that came to the forefront because greedy assholes had decided it was time to fulfill an agreement created over a century ago in Greece.

"What, exactly, do you think I will do to her?" I asked.

The "her" we spoke of was my fiancée, a woman I'd never

met, only seen a few pictures of, and had no intention of marrying, money be damned.

However, I wouldn't let these dicks know it.

When a courier had delivered a message this morning with a request for a meeting with the heads of the Mykos Shipping empire, I'd known it would be an interesting day.

My would-be future in-laws and I weren't the typical businessmen. We ran organizations, or let's say, families, with generational histories. Ones tied by deals, feuds, marriages, and so forth from the times when everyone lived in Europe— Greece, specifically, in our case.

Moving to the United States had eased some of the old-world views, but not all of them. Especially when it came to running our enterprises.

If there was something to say about families like ours, we were traditionalist and patriarchal as fuck.

Hence the reason we were here. The first female born into the Mykos family in over one hundred years.

Olympia Nyx Mykos. My fucking fiancée.

I liked my life the way it was. Business was business, and personal was personal. Nothing comingled.

Then my idiot uncle had to open his fucking mouth, reminding the world the Mykoses had finally produced a female offspring, and it was my obligation to marry the girl in order to end the century-long feud.

And, of course, the feud was caused by the last Mykos female because she decided to run away with her bodyguard, or chauffeur, or whatever the hell he was, instead of marrying my great-grandfather.

Now here I was, sitting in one of the most exclusive suites of a boutique hotel in Manhattan, trying to get to the bottom of whatever these fuckers wanted from me.

"You have a reputation, Drakos."

As if Tyler Mykos was all innocence and sunshine. Back in our college days, we'd shared a woman or two plenty of times.

Dickhead.

Tyler sat next to his father, Phillip Mykos, and his other three brothers, Evan, Damon, and Nico. He posed as Phillip's second, but everyone knew the truth. The eldest of the Mykos brothers was the power behind the Mykos shipping and syndicate empire. Nothing happened without his say-so, and this meeting was every inch Tyler's way of conducting business.

No formal offices of any kind, only private suites in high-end hotels, with five-star service while negotiating business terms.

They thought this little show of power could intimidate me. They'd better get their shit together. When one was raised under the thumb of a son-of-a-bitch grandfather like Giorgos "Gio" Astros Drakos, it was rare that anything could frighten a man.

"Why don't you enlighten me on this reputation, Mykos."

"Your preference for convenient women who give you no trouble."

Oh yes, I knew all about my bride. No one would describe her as convenient. She was known as the Mykos Hellion for having a tongue as sharp as the blades she was reported to pull on people who stepped on her wrong side.

Though some of the shit I'd heard about her seemed so off the wall, it wouldn't surprise me if these assholes planted the information to keep people away from her.

"Are you saying your sister is going to be a troublesome wife?"

"Not all of the rumors about her are true." Tyler's tone grew cool, telling me I'd pushed a button.

Meaning some were.

"Spell it out for me, Mykos."

"At the end of the year, she better be in the same state she is now."

Was he implying his sister was a virgin?

Were twenty-six-year-olds innocent nowadays? Maybe with the type of protection these guys probably had around her. But if she was the rebel everyone believed, I'd highly doubt it.

Though, I had no plans to find out otherwise. That road ensured these assholes remained a permanent part of my life.

"And what state is that?"

Phillip Mykos spoke this time. "Happy. If my baby girl sheds a tear because of you, I will make sure your world burns."

The way he held my gaze told me he meant every word.

Well, well, well. Wasn't that interesting.

The last thing anyone would ever believe of Phillip Mykos or his four sons was that they worried about the happiness of anyone else.

Then again, it had taken over one hundred years for a female to come from the Mykos line, and it would make sense for a woman to be their greatest weakness.

"I have no intention of making your daughter's life hard. This is a business arrangement between us. As long as your daughter and I understand each other, we will have a pleasant future together."

"That is where you're wrong."

4

The hell it was. We weren't ever going to be some happy family.

"Meaning?"

"Meaning my sister is personal. You fuck with her, you fuck with us. Therefore, it's personal until the engagement ends."

"First of all, what is it you think I'll do to her?" I leaned forward, ready to wipe the threat from the smug shit's face. "And second of all, what makes you think I will end this engagement? The contract states she's mine. You gain half the trust, except her portion of it, which will go into a new trust for our children. It's a win-win for me."

Tyler met my challenge, ready to push up from his seat. "Listen, asshole. You don't want her any more than she wants you. Everyone knows about your perfectly chosen bride waiting in the wings."

Before I could say anything, Phillip set a hand on Tyler's arm and rose from his seat, taking a set of folders from one of his men before passing one to me.

"We have an offer that will make it worth your while to break things off with my daughter at the end of the engagement term stated in the original contract between our elders."

Settling back in my chair, I glanced at Kasen Alexandros, my cousin and my second-in-command. He shrugged and then scanned the contents of the papers.

As I skimmed my own documents, I couldn't believe what I was reading.

Were these fuckers for real?

This was the last thing I expected when I walked into this hotel suite.

For years, I'd been trying to purchase a long-haul cargo port in Cypress to no avail, only to find out later a conglomerate of Mykos Shipping owned it and would never sell to anyone with a Drakos name.

"You're using the very port that you refused to sell me for the last five years as incentive to walk away from your daughter?"

"My empire is strong without it." Phillip shrugged. "You, on the other hand, can benefit from it tenfold. We will sign over our port in Cypress the second the trust clears and the engagement officially ends."

When my grandfather, Pappous Gio, had died in a helicopter crash a little over ten years ago, he'd left me a shipping conglomerate and territory poised for a hostile takeover. At twenty-three, I'd taken up the reins and, with the help of a few key allies, had fixed the mess my grandfather had created.

Today, Drakos Shipping stood strong enough to take on the Mykos empire, even if its patriarch believed otherwise.

"Tell me, what is it you think I will do to your precious Olympia if I marry her?"

"Her name is Nyx. Call her Olympia, and you're likely to get a blade to the throat," Evan, the youngest of the Mykoses, interjected with a tinge of humor rarely heard out of any of the brothers in public.

Deciding to rephrase the question, I asked, "Why are you so determined to keep me from marrying her?"

"Our world isn't right for her," Phillip answered. "She needs her freedom. You're not the man for her."

I studied the old man I'd viewed as a cold, calculating bastard my whole life. So many times, I'd wondered if he even had a heart. Especially when stories reached me of his detached, almost surgical means of information extraction from those who crossed him. He ran his empire with an iron fist, or the better words were "honed blade," and he'd taught his children all of his methods.

Well, more than likely the brothers were the ones who'd taught Olympia—correction, *Nyx*—her noted skills with knives. I highly doubted Phillip, with his overprotectiveness of his daughter's happiness, would want her doing anything in such an unrefined realm.

The fact he was showing this side of himself to me said his daughter truly meant a hell of a lot more to him than just a bargaining chip for alliances.

Might as well let him know they were off the hook. It would make the next year a hell of a lot easier.

"On that, we are in agreement. As she isn't the woman for me."

"Then you accept our terms."

"I have one term to add."

All five of the Mykos men narrowed identical gazes and waited.

"I want your backing when I take out the one who killed my parents and orchestrated my grandfather's helicopter crash."

"So, you figured it out, did you?" Phillip asked with a slight nod. "It's a hard lesson to learn who to trust."

"I figured it out years ago. I needed to put the chips into play."

"Is that so? Giving him enough rope to hang himself?"

"Exactly."

"I always knew you were more like Ky than Gio. It must

have pissed your grandfather off to hell and back to know he couldn't beat his errant son out of you."

His words felt like a punch to the gut, knowing how wrong they were.

I was my grandfather's creation. Everything he couldn't get from my father, Kyros, he'd molded into me, sometimes with a belt or fist.

My father was the second son, the one who shouldn't have inherited the empire but had because his brother had died in a territory war. He had been the son who'd shunned responsibility and married a woman of his choice instead of his dead brother's fiancée to keep a family alliance. The son Pappous couldn't control. When my parents had been killed in a car crash, my grandfather got a do-over—me.

I gave no reaction to Mykos's statement and instead asked, "So, do I have your support?"

"Yes," Tyler answered for Phillip. "We don't like traitors in our midst, especially when they're family. You follow our terms, we follow yours."

I nodded. "In a little over one year's time, I will break the marriage contract, we will split the trust, and you will hand over the port. Then, when I call on your backing, you will show up to take out the trash."

"Excellent." Tyler lifted a glass of wine to his lips, took a deep swallow, and then said, "One more thing."

I waited.

"No one outside of the people in this room will know about this arrangement." The order in Tyler's tone grated on my last nerve.

"What about Nyx?"

Nico spoke for the first time. "Obviously, she will find out. This does concern her life, after all."

"What you're leaving out is that she has no idea we are meeting now. Why?"

"There was no point in saying anything until we had your agreement."

I studied the men. They were most definitely keeping something from me. Whatever it was, I planned to find out.

"I see. Is that the last stipulation for our agreement?" I asked, ready to get the hell out of the hotel and on the road to catch the flight waiting for me in the hangar at JFK.

"It is. One year from the date of the official engagement we will meet again and finalize everything." Tyler stood, offering me his hand.

Rising from my seat, I shook his hand. "Now, gentlemen, I have another meeting to attend. I will see you in three months' time, at my engagement party."

Without another word, I moved to the door.

I waited to speak until Kasen and I were in my car and my men were following behind me. I couldn't trust any of the Mykoses not to have men stationed around the hotel property.

"I want anything and everything on Nyx Mykos. They are too fucking protective of her happiness for my taste."

"We're already watching her. She's clean as an angel. For the last month, we've watched her day and night. All she does is play with her plants, hang out with her cousins, and have her bodyguards shadow her. She's boring as hell. I'm beginning to think she was a target of those socialite bitches and that's why she moved to Vegas."

It was possible. Anyone who refused to conform to the

standards of our world suffered the ramifications of the majority, especially the women. Being different wasn't a good thing. And Nyx Mykos marched to the beat of her own drum.

But then again, my gut said that line of thought was all bullshit. And my gut had never let me down.

Well, I'd find out soon enough.

It was time for one last meeting, one to set the rules for the next year.

With my fiancée.

I couldn't help but smile.

Her invitation had arrived in a similar fashion as her brother's, but more upfront, to the point, and with the complete confidence that I'd fly across the country on such short notice.

I have an offer you can't refuse to end our engagement.

To learn the details, meet me at 7 p.m. tonight @ Epieikeia.

Ida Hotel and Casino, Las Vegas.

Her sheer balls made her proposal irresistible. It had been a long fucking time since anyone had piqued my curiosity.

And in the way my men and Kasen seemed so enamored of her, it made it more than imperative to find out if she was the nature nymph or the New York hellion.

"When you meet her, are you going to let her know about the deal with her family or are you going to string her along to see what she offers?"

"What do you think?"

Kasen shook his head. "I think this is going to blow up in your face. Don't fuck with her, she's an innocent. Plus, you need her family as much as they need you."

"No Mykos is innocent."

"This one is."

"Stop worrying. By the time her family tells her about our agreement, we will have established our ground rules."

"Let me guess. No scandals, no trouble, no fucking around."

"I'm the one with the power of the morality clause to my benefit. Her family loses everything if she doesn't stay in line. Might as well make it clear."

"As I said, you won't have any problem with any of this. She is nothing like the rumors."

"Then it won't be any problem to reiterate it."

"Wouldn't it make your life easier for the next year to have a fiancée who likes you versus one who hates you?"

"This is business. I don't care how she feels about me as long as I have the money and my agreement with her family stands."

"Famous last words."

2

NYX

"OLYMPIA NYX MYKOS, YOU MUST GET MARRIED. DO YOU HEAR me?" my cousin-in-law Penny Lykaios mocked in an exaggerated Greek accent as she cocked a hand on her hip and tossed her high ponytail of long black hair to the side.

"No. I'd rather become a nun and move into a convent." I folded my arms, trying not to laugh and sling dirt everywhere from the potting soil on my gloves.

I was covered in all kinds of plant life, tinged with sweat from the balmy ninety-degree heat in the botanical gardens of the Ida Hotel and Casino in Las Vegas, and I couldn't imagine being anywhere else.

"It is your duty to fulfill the contract. Our family is depending on that money." Penny pursed her lips and picked up a hybrid tulip to transfer into its new home, making a pretty good impression of the disappointed scowl my Aunt Teresa gave me every time she looked in my direction.

"I didn't make the contract. I don't have to do anything."

Penny harrumphed and tossed her hair, slinging a giant wad of dirt above us and making it so hard for me to keep a snort inside. "You are shaming the family. First, you move to Las Vegas to live with those Lykaios heathens who gamble and drink all day, and now this. That Penny Lykaios is a bad influence—a good Greek girl wouldn't spend her days making liquor. What was your father thinking?"

Neither of us could keep a straight face anymore, and we both fell on our butts, laughing hysterically.

The tourists observing us from the observation side of the gardens probably thought we were complete morons. Thankfully, it was right before the back rooms closed for viewing, and only a few people were milling about at this time of the early evening.

After a few more moments of uncontrollable laughter, we gathered some semblance of professionalism and righted ourselves.

"Damn, you do a fabulous impression of Aunt Teresa. She's so worried I'm going to run away that she forgets I'm the one stuck in this contract."

"It's the money she wants. She doesn't actually care what happens to you."

Yes, the money.

Not just a small chunk of change. An amount totaling well over a billion dollars. It sounded insane when I thought about it, but a century of interest compounding in a Swiss trust could do wonders.

If only my great-aunt Julia hadn't fallen in love with her bodyguard and run away from her arranged marriage, I wouldn't be in this situation.

Then again, I couldn't really begrudge her for picking love over money. Plus, I'd seen pictures of my great-uncle Victor Danos, and he was smokin' hot.

Like movie-star, mafia-romance-novel sizzling.

"Money is all anyone ever wants. If I'd been born a boy, the trust would have sat for another generation or two," I muttered to myself as I jabbed my trowel into the flowerbed to shovel some soil aside.

"Count your blessings. At least your family ignored your aunts and uncles' backward views on women and didn't have any objections to you becoming a horticulturist or moving to Vegas."

If she only knew the hoops I'd jumped through to even pursue a degree at NYU. The only reason I'd gotten my master's and PhD was that it was an all-in-one undergraduate-to-graduate program I'd worked my ass off to qualify for. Not to mention the hours it took to convince Papa that moving to Vegas and taking over the botanical gardens at the Ida, a casino owned by Mama's cousin, my deceased Aunt Rhea's sons and daughter, was an opportunity of a lifetime.

"Let's say there were a lot of compromises, but my brothers had my back."

I smiled thinking of Tyler, Nico, Damon, and Evan. They understood that I wasn't meant for the role I was born into. Under their tutelage, I'd learned skills no proper Greek girl should know, from how to win fistfights and shoot guns, to wielding a knife in such a precise manner, it would leave the least amount of blood splatter.

Yeah, when I thought about it, my upbringing wasn't normal by any family's standards, syndicate or not.

"You're the debutante who can count cards and wield a blade like a ninja. No wonder my boys love their Auntie Nyx so much."

"Hey, I resent that. I never cheat. I just know the tricks to keep others from taking advantage of me. It comes in handy living in Vegas."

"And your love of knives?"

"I don't play with those anymore, remember? It was part of my bargain with my brothers. It's no longer my thing."

"Who are you kidding? If it's something that will make your family freak out, it's your thing."

"I won't deny it." I shrugged. "Though, nowadays, the tables are where my vices lay."

I'd learned the etiquette of a proper lady, but if it was taboo, I was drawn to it.

Especially gambling.

Poker. Blackjack. Roulette. You name it, I played it. And I won. Big.

That was one of the many reasons I never, ever wanted to leave Vegas.

One day, I would find my own damn man. Someone who accepted me with all my crazy quirks and wouldn't expect me to fit into some fucking mold. He wouldn't be a predetermined, stuffy, follow-the-rules, with backward views man.

"Are you really going to go through with this crazy plan of yours? I'm not sure it's going to work."

Brushing a stray hair from my forehead with my arm, I sighed. "What choice do I have? It's that or accept that I'm the future Mrs. Simon Christopher Drakos."

"Your plan hangs on the hope he doesn't want to marry you. Remember, he's the one who makes out big if the wedding goes through."

"I know for a fact I'm not his ideal mate. Men like him want a calm, perfect socialite, and I'm definitely not her."

"Let's not forget all of those clauses in the contract. You have to hold to a strict code of morality. You're in deep shit if he ever learns of your underground activities."

Deep shit was an understatement.

Not only would my family lose their shit in the worst possible way, if they learned I ran an underground, high-stakes poker club that netted millions, but my betrothed could use it to steal the whole fucking trust from my family. According to the fine print of the insane contract, I had to show that I lived a pure life without a hint of scandal to shame my future husband.

What a crock of back-assed bullshit.

I clenched my teeth. "It pisses me off that he's free to do whatever he wants with whomever he wants, whenever he wants. And I'm stuck in limbo. Fuck that shit. Men suck."

"Well, they have their uses." Penny smirked. "Or, certain parts of them do."

"I wouldn't know since I have to live a chaste life, remember?"

"You're such a liar. Your bestie ratted you out before she left town last week. How many men have you turned down for some reason or another?"

I really wanted to strangle my best friend, Akari. I couldn't wait until we met up tonight. I was so going to let her have it.

The woman talked too much, and I knew when she planned a night out with Penny and my other cousins-in-law, it would only lead to unnecessary gossip.

Bitch knew girl code meant not talking about my love life or lack thereof to my nosy cousins.

"I'm selective. I can't deal with the typical Vegas guys. They annoy me."

"What you need is someone who won't let you intimidate him."

"I don't intimidate anyone. I play with plants all day."

"And run a den of illegal card games at night while holding honed knives to the throats of anyone who cheats."

"The threat of it is scarier than doing it. Plus, I have people to take care of that shit."

"You just proved my point. You intimidate the hell out of the average guy."

"I have never uttered the words, 'I want an average guy.'"

"But you did say you didn't want one from your world."

"And here I am, engaged to one. This has to be some cruel joke."

"I still can't believe all of this started because Drakos's uncle decided to push to enforce the contract."

I sighed. "Money is a great motivator. Look at Aunt Teresa—she jumped on the train as soon as she heard how much was involved."

"Just to play devil's advocate, what if he wants to marry you?"

"I'll convince him otherwise. I can't go back to New York. Vegas is where I belong. This is where I fit."

"Is it really that bad?"

"Every time I go home, I feel as if I'm being put in a cage. All these rules, all these expectations. Every move I make is watched. I'm the first Mykos female born in over a hundred years. I'm like a prize horse everyone wants to buy. Then add on the pressure to be perfect."

"So, you show everyone how imperfect you are and make them run as fast as possible away from you." Penny lifted a brow.

"I guess."

"Doesn't that get exhausting too?"

"More than you can imagine. Hence the reason I never want to go back. I can be myself here. People don't have expectations of me based on rules of the past. I'm not bound by archaic principles of behavior."

"Then I suggest you talk to your family, meaning your parents and brothers, before you go through with this plan of yours. I have a feeling Simon Drakos isn't going to sway as easily as you hope."

"I can't do that. What am I going to say? Sorry, Papa, I hate the life you gave me and want nothing to do with it. Yes, I know it's very privileged, and I probably sound like a spoiled brat. But you see, being a Greek syndicate boss's daughter is too stifling. So would you mind pretending I wasn't part of the family so I can live in peace in Vegas?"

Just the thought of uttering any of those words made me cringe inside. I couldn't say anything like that to Papa. Plus, I couldn't truly live without my family. They were a deep-rooted part of me.

"Phillip Mykos is known for making grown men cry and more. He can handle it."

"That's the thing. He's not as cruel and cold as everyone believes. Papa is really sensitive."

Penny stared at me as if I'd lost my mind.

What she couldn't understand was that Papa was a hard-ass in all things except when it came to Mama and me. Cherishing his women, as he called it, was his life's mission. We were his soft spot. And if I went without a trip home at least every three weeks, he'd fall into a mini depression.

"His nickname is the Mykos Surgeon. That's like saying my giant of a husband is a warm, huggable teddy bear. You know that's the furthest thing from the truth. Hagen can scare the shit out of people with just a stare."

"I'm offended, Starlight. You seem to enjoy certain giant aspects of my body." A deep voice spoke from behind us, and immediately Penny's cheeks were tinged with a hue of pink.

"True. And hence the reason I was pregnant or nursing for six years in a row."

I wanted to roll my eyes, but if I was honest with myself, I adored how Penny and Hagen interacted. The two never seemed to get enough of each other.

This was the case with all of the Lykaioses and their wives and the same for my other cousin, Ana, who was Hagen's half-sister and married to Penny's brother, Ian.

Yep, it was a crazy hot Greek mess of relationships, but it worked for us.

"Is there a reason you're here, dear cousin?" I asked Hagen.

"Penny and I were having girl talk as we transplanted some new tulips."

"I've come to take my wife away. The kids are having quality time with their cousins this weekend, so I have my wife all to myself."

Immediately, Penny jumped up. "Sorry, this is a priority. We don't get many opportunities like this. If one of the brothers decided to take my boys for the weekend, I'm going to make use of the opportunity."

"I see how it is. Leaving me for sex and food."

"Exactly." Penny smiled over her shoulder and then tucked her arm into the crook of Hagen's.

Hagen gazed down at Penny with something that I could only describe as reverence. Even after a decade together, he always seemed so in awe that he'd married his dream girl.

Never would I have thought Hagen, the cold-as-ice former mob-enforcer-turned-hotel-magnate, would fall head over heels in love with a pint-sized, takes-no-one's-shit whiskey maker.

Sometimes opposites were the perfect match.

Maybe one day I'd find my ideal partner.

And for that to come to fruition, I had to convince Simon Drakos to free me from this engagement.

It really sucked that he had the ability to end things but I couldn't.

What the ever-loving fuck?

I adored my Greek culture, but some of those old traditionalist aspects really pissed me off.

Then again, it had been my great-aunt who'd run away, and so they'd put into place an extra clause making it impossible for the bride to do anything but show up to the wedding without it costing her family everything.

My phone beeped, giving me the signal to wrap up my work and head to my apartment in the Ida residential tower. I had a long evening ahead of me and needed to prepare.

First was a meeting with my hopefully temporary fiancé. Then I'd meet up with my ride-or-die, Akari Ota.

Tomorrow I'd spend my day conducting in-depth research, from debt history to reputation among business associates, for prospective game-night attendees.

This was another reason I needed to get out of this asinine marriage contract. No way in hell would I give up a business I'd built from the ground up. And that was exactly what Simon Drakos would expect me to do as soon as he learned of any aspect of my venture.

He couldn't really want to marry me, could he? The Mykos Hellion?

God, I was giving myself a headache stressing about this.

Releasing a deep breath, I pushed the thoughts to the back of my mind and gathered all of my tools.

Once I had placed them on the cart near me, I set my hand on the edge to stand, but the cart rolled, and I lost my balance.

Before I could catch myself, I fell onto my knees.

Fucking fabulous.

Wiping the sweat and soil from my face, I sighed.

Looking at me now, no one would believe I was anything more than a clumsy nerd in a garden. Then again, I wouldn't lie and say I hadn't used this misconception to my advantage, letting others underestimate me.

It kept people from snooping too deeply. If the truth about

my extracurricular activities ever got out, it could cause a whole world of trouble. Some things were better kept in the dark.

Maybe one day, I'd find someone to share all of my secrets, someone who accepted the wildness in me, someone who wouldn't try to tame me.

Leveraging myself up against the viewing glass, I shifted back onto my heels. Just as I was about to stand, my eyes connected with piercing green ones.

My pulse jumped, starting a hammering beat in my chest, and a shiver shot down my spine as goosebumps prickled my skin. I couldn't seem to move, as if I were frozen in place, and this crackle of energy surged between us.

Holy shit.

Who the fuck was he?

This definitely wasn't the typical Vegas hot guy on vacation I encountered on a daily basis. The type of tourist who thought he could impress a local girl with a great body and good looks.

This man oozed a potent mix of sex and confidence that told any woman who dared venture in his direction he was dangerous but definitely worth the walk on the wicked side.

The hint of tattoos peeking from his designer shirt added to his bad-boy vibe, and I had no doubt a honed, muscled body lay under the clothes he wore.

Arousal flooded my cleft as my nipples hardened to stiff peaks, and the urge to press my thighs together prickled at the back of my mind.

He stepped closer to the glass dividing us and continued to hold my stare in the way that made it impossible for me to shift my gaze.

My breath grew shallow, and the low throbbing deep in my core intensified.

Fuck. What was happening to me? And why was his face familiar? I couldn't know him, could I?

No, this was the type of man a woman conjured in her fantasies. The ones she'd never take a chance on in reality.

I licked my lips, hypnotized by the darkening of his irises.

It was as if he possessed some type of thrall connected directly to my libido.

Never had I responded to anyone this way.

I swallowed, trying to quench my parched throat.

That was when he mouthed the words, "Come outside, and we can talk."

He wanted to what?

Talk?

Clearing the haze, I shook my head and responded, "No."

This guy had trouble written all over him. The last thing I needed was anything to overwhelm an already complicated life. No matter how tempting the thought of a dance with a devil was at the moment.

And he was all things bad and indulgent.

He nodded *yes*.

Before I could say no again, a throat cleared behind me, breaking the trance the sexy-as-sin man had weaved around me.

I turned to find the head of my personal security, Stevie Nem, staring at me with a knowing glint in her eyes and a smug set to her lips.

"Time to prepare for your evening. No more sightseeing."

I returned my focus to the window. The stranger had

disappeared, leaving me with a sense of both disappointment and relief.

"I believe you just saved me from succumbing to a very bad decision." I rose to my feet and then brushed the soil from my clothes, feeling as if I'd missed the opportunity of a lifetime.

"That's why you pay me the big bucks. I keep the riffraff away."

"Boy, did that riffraff look so deliciously tempting."

3

SIMON

"WHAT THE FUCK WAS THAT?" I ASKED MYSELF AS I GRIPPED THE back of my neck and made my way into the main thoroughfare through Ida's casino.

I'd known better than to let my curiosity get the best of me, but my need to see the Mykos Hellion in her natural element had gotten the best of me, and instead of checking in to my suite, I'd detoured to the Ida botanical gardens.

What I hadn't expected was my body's visceral reaction to the innocent-appearing woman with dirt covering her face and big dark eyes that drew a man in with a simple glance. Or the natural cover-model beauty she possessed with the barest of makeup on her skin.

For nearly twenty minutes, I observed her as she laughed

and chatted with Persephone Lykaios, completely relaxed and without an ounce of pretension. Nowhere was the snarky, cutting bitch attitude people in New York reported her as having. She seemed so full of life, joy, innocence, and at times, mischief.

She'd completely captivated me, making it impossible to take my gaze away from her.

If it wasn't for the signature Mykos onyx eyes, I'd never have believed she was my fiancée. And the sick bastard part of me itched to corrupt every fucking inch of her.

Get it together, asshole. She isn't for you.

Touching her would come at a price, one I refused to pay, no matter the delicious, curvy, goddess package she came in.

How the fuck had my men thought she was boring? Were they blind?

I made my way through the lobby of the Ida and toward the private suites tower of the hotel. Just as I reached the bank of elevators, Kasen stepped out from the shadows.

The humor in the green eyes that were so much like mine gave me the urge to clock him in the jaw. He'd watched the interplay between Nyx and me and was getting a kick out of it.

The dickhead knew me better than most people. He'd been the one source of fun Pappous had allowed in my life growing up. To this day, he was the only man I could count on to always have my back.

Kasen was the son of Aunt Dalani, my father's twin. My aunt had done everything my grandfather had expected of her, including marrying the right man from the right family with the right background. And because Aunt Dalani had followed the rules dictated for her life, Pappous considered Kasen a good influence.

Luckily for my aunt, Uncle Steven happened to be her high school boyfriend and not someone forced upon her.

"Were the reports right or wrong?"

They were fucking wrong—none of them remotely indicated she was drop-dead gorgeous.

Instead of giving him my actual thoughts, I thought out loud, "She has to have secrets. No one is that fucking pure."

Or gave a man visions of everything he wanted to do to her in bed.

Kasen's lips turned up at the corner. "She's your type. I fucking knew it."

Ignoring him, I stalked to the elevator cab, stepped inside, and punched the button to our private floor.

It took all my effort not to wipe the smirk off Kasen's face.

"I don't have a type."

"I call bullshit. Dark hair, dark eyes, and a body with curves in all the right places. The only difference from your regular MO is that she's smart and has a bunch of letters after her name. Isn't she some type of doctor?"

"PhD. The women I see aren't idiots."

"She's still a type of doctor, even if she's not an MD. The women you see put up with your bullshit. Smart women don't have time for assholes. Maybe that's why she gets a bad rap."

Fucker thought he was so funny.

"When did you become her advocate?"

"I'm telling you like it is. I trust our men, and they like her. Plus"—he paused for a second, making me think I was going to hate what he had to say—"I watched your reaction to her. You want her."

That was the fucking problem.

"You're an asshole."

"No, that's your reputation. You know, 'the master of fortune and darkness' shit. I'm the sidekick who cleans up the carnage after you lay down the law."

If he wasn't one of the few people I trusted with my life, I'd have killed him years ago.

Kasen seemed to garner great joy out of reminding me of the bogeyman reputation I'd developed after I'd taken over my grandfather's position in Drakos Shipping.

I'd followed in Pappous's footsteps and created fear in those who'd thought I was too weak to hold my family's organization together. I'd made it a point to take back everything stolen from my family and then some.

"Seriously, what's the big deal with seeing where things go?"

"Touching her is the last thing I should do. The consequences are too great."

"The worst consequences would be that you're married to a smoking-hot and smart woman, and the Mykoses go from rivals to allies."

Ignoring his words, I moved out of the elevator and into the hallway leading directly to my suite.

"You know I'm right."

Shooting Kasen a glare, I moved straight to a stocked bar. "The woman I'll marry isn't going to have a rep, as you put it, of any kind. I need someone who understands what's expected of her, not a hellion giving me trouble at every turn."

"You mean someone you can manage, like Santos's daughter.

She won't give you any problems. She'll keep her opinions to herself, stay hidden away, and only come out for events as long as you let her stay busy spending your money."

When he put it that way, I sounded like a right bastard.

Then again, it wasn't as if Camilla Santos wasn't aware of the life she'd live. She liked the money and influence as much as the next woman.

Well, maybe not Nyx Mykos.

An image of her dark eyes flashed in my mind, of her kneeling before me, of her mouth wrapped around my cock.

Fuck.

I clenched my teeth. I had to get it together. Of all the women in the world to have an immediate physical reaction to, it had to be her. Even Wes Santos's daughter, a well-known beauty, never gave me visions of fucking her senseless with barely one interaction.

I poured two fingers of scotch into a tumbler, picked up the glass, and shot back the potent liquid, letting the alcohol burn down my throat.

"It's too late to take our dear Uncle Albert out. If you'd done it ten years ago, you wouldn't be in this situation."

Kasen's emphasis on the "uncle" part had me shaking my head. We never called him uncle. Fucker, bastard, dickhead, and waste of space, yes. But not uncle.

"He'll get his, sooner or later."

Albert was the second spare, as Pappous had called him, and because of this designation, he carried a perpetual chip on his shoulder. He wanted what his older brothers had but without putting in the effort. I'd seen it as a child and saw it in full force when he tried to pull rank after I'd taken over the family. Too bad age had nothing to do with succession of the family.

I'd learned the business the hard way, not by playing errand boy or living off the profits.

The fucker had no idea I knew all about his involvement in the helicopter crash that killed Pappous. Though the intended target had never made the flight.

Me.

It was Pappous's need to control every contract negotiation that had him replacing me on the flight that day.

Now here I was, dealing with more of Albert's bullshit.

Up until a few months ago, I'd never bothered worrying about the archaic contract my great-grandfather had concocted. No one in the modern era expected anyone to honor a deal made in Greece over a hundred years ago.

Then Albert decided he wanted more of the Drakos pie and pushed the family elders to enforce the Mykos-Drakos agreement.

Maybe Kasen was right. I should have killed the backstabbing bastard when I'd had the chance a decade ago.

"Your only option is to stick it out for the next year and deal with the consequences."

"There aren't going to be any consequences."

"You're too smart to believe that bullshit. You may not have any intention of marrying Nyx Mykos, but I guarantee you're going to end up in bed within the next month. And that's where the consequences are going to fuck you up."

"Let me repeat, there aren't going to be any consequences. After all, she is my fiancée. And that puts us in an exclusive club for the next twelve months. And membership has its privileges."

"You're going to fuck this up royally."

"My gut says she isn't as innocent as all of you believe. She can handle me. While I go negotiate with my fiancée, I want you to keep digging. We leave Monday morning. You have three days."

4

NYX

I ENTERED EPIEIKEIA, THE GREEK-INSPIRED CAFE KNOWN FOR ITS
sweet pastries, around six forty-five with Tony and two of my
security detail close behind me. My stomach churned as I
steeled myself for any and every outcome of my meeting with
Simon Drakos, including the dreaded prospect I'd have to
marry him and return to New York.

And lose my freedom.

"Ms. Mykos, I have your table ready," Jesse, the hostess,
informed me as I approached. "We've placed you in the private
dining area, and as per your request, outside of your server, no
one will disturb you."

"Thank you so much for arranging this."

Jesse smiled as she led me to my corner of the restaurant.

"It's the least I could do for helping me out with my botany classes."

Once I was seated and Jesse left, Tony leaned forward, took my hand, and placed a small disk in my palm.

"We will wait by the bar for you. Just give us the signal and I'll come get you. I don't give a shit who he is. You want out, I'll get you out."

It was the emergency alert connected to his phone designed to signal I was ready to leave a place without causing a scene. Tony never took any chances with my safety, no matter who I met, friend or foe. And in his eyes, Simon Drakos qualified as foe.

"He's my fiancé. Technically, we aren't supposed to be anywhere near each other until the official engagement. He isn't going to do anything that will cause a problem."

"If you believe that line of bullshit, I have a bridge to sell you, Silent Night."

I narrowed my eyes, understanding his reminder that my underground club activities were at stake if things went south with my hopefully temporary fiancé.

"Speaking of Silent Night. Have the invitations gone out?"

"Yes."

"Affirmatives?

"All but one."

"Who?"

"The same one, as usual."

My lips curved up at the corners. "He just wants the invite. I think if he ever showed up, half the room would pee themselves."

"Only you would think of him as a sweet grandfather type."

33

I lifted a brow. "People say the same thing about Papa and my brothers. I'm not blind to who they are. I just accept them."

"But they sure are blind to who you are."

I shrugged. "That's why I need this to work. Once this year is out, I can explain everything. Make them understand that I don't ever want to go back."

"Then for your sake, let's hope Simon Drakos doesn't live up to the asshole reputation he's known for."

"Did you really have to say that?"

"I'm not here to give you false hope. I keep it real."

"Thanks a lot."

"Anytime." He stepped away and took his position at the bar where he could keep his sights on me and the expanse of the whole dining area without obstruction.

Over the next fifteen minutes, I ordered some sparkling water, sipped my drink, and scrolled through the news on my phone.

No matter how hard I tried, I couldn't push away the anxiety lying like a heavy weight in the pit of my stomach.

This had to work. I couldn't go back. New York wasn't the place for me anymore.

Guilt hit my heart.

It wasn't a bad life. But it was one where I had no say. There were rules for everything. What to do. What to wear. What to say. I was the girl with the temper, who liked to play in the dirt, the one who threw knives and said the wrong things.

Yes, I liked my pretty things and playing dress-up, but I never wanted it to become part of my day-to-day existence.

Then there was my gambling vice.

What would my family do if they ever learned I'd run

underground casino nights all through college and graduate school and that it wasn't something new I'd learned in Vegas?

Hell, what would my intended think?

Fuck. I'd thought the word *intended*. This engagement shit was getting to me.

Closing my eyes, I took in a few steadying breaths to clear my mind and calm my thoughts. However, instead of accomplishing those goals, the image of the man with the piercing emerald gaze flashed to the forefront.

Yep, and then there was that guy.

Of all the days to have anyone affect my body, it had to happen today. I'd waited for five fucking years for someone to make me want to throw caution to the wind, to make it worth stepping out of the box, and in a matter of a few seconds and with a look, this random man who I hadn't even uttered a word to had me craving to let him do every dirty, wicked thing I'd seen in his eyes.

Maybe this was some cruel joke by the Greek gods for being the rebel Mykos.

A shiver slid down my spine, and I opened my lids, finding the very devil standing across the room.

Oh, fuck me. This was bad.

Please don't notice me. Please don't notice me.

Shit. Too late.

His focus locked with mine, and my heartbeat accelerated into a rapid roaring rhythm in my ears. An immediate ache ignited between my legs, making the desire I'd experienced earlier mild compared to what was coursing through my body now.

"Stay right there," he mouthed as he set a course in my

direction, not pausing when Jesse tried to intercept him, and weaved his way among the multitude of tables separating us.

He'd changed into slacks and a tailored jacket. The dark blue shirt he wore was open at the collar, revealing the black tattoos crawling up the back of his neck. There was no hiding the fact a honed, sculpted body lay under all of those clothes.

The complete confidence with the way he carried himself and kept me in his sights gave me the feeling of a predator who was stalking his next meal.

"Olympia Nyx Mykos," he stated as he stopped at my table. The deep rasp of his voice washed over me and shot straight to my core.

I tilted my head up, taking him in. He seemed so much larger than when he stood on the other side of the observation glass.

His presence was overwhelming, almost too much.

Wait. He'd said Olympia. No one in Vegas called me Olympia. Hell, most people hadn't a clue my name was anything other than Nyx.

Who the fuck was this guy?

"How do you know my name?"

"Shouldn't I know my fiancée's name?"

Wait. *Fiancée?*

Oh, dear God. What the fuck was happening? No this couldn't be right.

"What?" A dizziness filled my head, and I grabbed hold of the edge of the table. "You're Simon Drakos?"

The intense way he held my gaze increased the arousal already coursing inside me and made me want to smack myself.

"I am. And I believe our negotiations for your freedom are about to get very interesting."

I clenched my teeth, and the haze of lust from seconds earlier dimmed.

Was he for real? He couldn't be implying what I thought he was implying.

"You don't want to marry me any more than I want to marry you. Why don't you take a seat and listen to my offer? If you don't like what I have to say, you can fuck off, and I'm in no worse a position than I was a second ago."

"If that's how you want to play it." He pulled out the chair across the table from me and sat. "We'll do it your way. Just know the ball is in my court."

"I don't play ball. My preferred game is cards. And in Vegas, the house always wins."

"Then deal, Ms. Mykos. What is your freedom from a life tied to me, in my bed, to do with as I will, worth?"

The heat in his hypnotic green irises had my core quivering in a way I'd never experienced before. The asshole was fucking potent, and he knew it.

I refused to look away. That was his goal—to intimidate me, to make me squirm, to make me feel as if he had all the power.

Trying to ignore the way my traitorous body responded to him, I stated, "One hundred million dollars."

"Are you offering me your share of the trust? Don't you need it?"

"I'd rather work for the rest of my life than spend my existence in a loveless marriage."

"Love is a fairytale the world brainwashes into little girls."

"My father loves my mother so I know it's not a fairytale," I

37

challenged, lifting my chin before adding, "And your parents eloped so obviously they had more than just a passing affection."

A crease formed between his brows. "What do you know of my parents?"

The hardening of his tone conveyed that I'd touched a nerve.

Interesting.

"I know what my mother told me. Your parents had a torrid affair, and your father turned his back on a lucrative marriage contract, a position with his father, and a fortune for your mother. If that's not love, what is?"

"Love makes people weak."

"So, you do believe in love but don't have time for the complications, is that it?"

"Love isn't something I care to pursue with anyone. Marriage, for me, is a mutually agreed-upon business arrangement."

"And hence the reason we aren't a match."

"So, you want love, roses, and happily ever after. It doesn't exist."

"I'm not naive. Love doesn't mean everything is perfect. It just means the couple accepts each other the way they are. They don't have to change to fit a mold or be something society says they have to become. Or hide away the deepest, darkest parts of themselves."

"What is it you want your future husband to accept about you, Nyx? What is it you hide from the world?" He leaned forward, using that thrall stare I'd experienced earlier in the day.

I licked my lips. "If you were the man I planned to marry, the one I loved, then I'd tell you. But you're not. I want to know, what is it going to take to end this one year from now?"

"You want my price for freeing you from this engagement—besides your portion of the trust, you mean?"

"Yes." I reached for my glass of water, but before I grabbed hold of it, he clasped his fingers around my forearm, sending a shockwave of sensation over my skin.

Holy shit, I shouldn't react to him like this.

"Let me go, Simon."

"No. We're in the middle of negotiations." He paused and then added with a smirk, "For your freedom."

He held my arm with one hand and drew lazy circles along the vein on the inside of my wrist with the fingertips of the other.

His touch sent shivers down my spine as if his fingers were livewires. My face heated, and my breath grew shallow.

"I'm not sleeping with you."

But if he were any other man looking at me the way he was, I would have jumped at the chance. I would have let him do all the dark and wicked things swimming in those emerald irises.

"Are you sure about that? I know you're attracted to me. I see it in the way your pupils dilate, the way your lips part to take in little breaths, the way the flush on your skin deepens as I stroke the skin on your arm."

Dear God, this man could seduce with just his words.

I swallowed, trying to ease my parched throat. "I don't sleep with every man I find attractive."

"The plan isn't to sleep, Nyx."

"It's not going to happen, Simon."

As if I hadn't spoken, he lifted my hand, bringing my wrist to his mouth. I watched in curious fascination as he grazed his teeth along my sensitive skin. And it took all my will not to moan.

Realizing he'd caught my reaction, I jerked my arm from his hold. "No."

"I don't think you're understanding how this works. You want your freedom, then for the next year, I want you in my bed. Whenever I want. However I want. To do with whatever I want."

The arrogant, insufferable asshole.

Where the fuck were my knives when I needed them?

Yes, I knew. Stevie told me I couldn't bring them since it wasn't civilized to threaten my fiancé with bodily harm. See where that got me?

The arousal from only moments earlier had all but disappeared as my temper flared to an inferno level.

Narrowing my gaze, I rose to my feet and cocked a hand on my hip. "Well, I have a response to your proposal, Mr. Drakos."

"What is that, Ms. Mykos?" He stood, meeting my challenge.

He towered his at least ten-inch height difference over me, pissing me off even further.

"You're an asshole, Simon Drakos," I seethed through clenched teeth, poking him in the chest, not caring that we were garnering curious glances from the patrons around us.

"I'm an asshole you're going to get to know very intimately."

"God, you are so damn cocky. If I had my knives right now, I'd—" I cut myself off, trying to rein in my temper.

"Would you gut me as those rumors say you would?" He stepped closer to me, capturing the hand that had just pushed him. "Just know, that isn't the type of edge play I normally engage in, but for you, I can make an exception."

I tugged at my hand, but he held it firm. "I'm not going to fuck you."

"Keep lying to yourself, Nyx Mykos. You knew it was inevitable from the moment our eyes connected in the gardens. You're just pissed that I am who I am."

"That's where you're wrong. I won't deny I'm attracted to you. But then again, Vegas is filled with good-looking men. I can scratch an itch whenever I want. I don't need you."

"Then why haven't you? From what I hear, you prefer plants to a real man."

"I'm selective. I'm not a whore to use and discard. You're just like all of them back home. You think you can fuck whoever you want. No, you're worse, since you have the looks to match the ego. So, I'll leave you with these final words."

"And they are?"

"You can take your counteroffer and fuck off." Turning, I stalked out of the restaurant.

5

SIMON

I WATCHED NYX STORM OUT OF THE RESTAURANT WITH HER security close behind her, and all I could think about was if her eyes would go as dark with passion as they had with anger.

Something I had every intention of finding out.

Yep, I couldn't deny it. I was the asshole she claimed I was.

Then again, Gio Drakos had molded me into his image, and he only viewed things from the lens of what worked for the Drakos family, meaning him.

"That went well," Kasen stated as he approached from my right. "I believe this is the first time I've ever seen anyone tell you to fuck off and walk away."

"Oh, she isn't walking away for long."

Kasen shook his head at me. "This is a seriously sadistic version of foreplay."

"I guess you would know since you're the sadist out of the two of us."

"At least I own my kinks."

"I don't need to label it to own it. I just need a woman to accept what I want and to do it."

"And you think your little fiancée is that woman."

"There is no think about it. I know." A smile tugged at my lips. "And what pisses her off the most is that she likes the idea of it too damn much."

I'd called her on the way her breaths changed and her eyes dilated. But she had no clue I'd noticed her attempt to anchor herself by gripping the edge of the table and the way she kept squirming because the arousal she felt between her legs made her ache.

"I know there is no point in warning you again."

"Then don't."

"However. It's my job to watch your back. So here it is: if you don't want to fuck up your agreement with Mykos, don't fuck his sister."

"Since you're so worried about my back, as you put it, I'll make a deal with you. As long as Nyx Mykos maintains her pure-as-driven-snow, blade-loving, morally superior illusion that seems to have captured all of your balls in a vise grip, I won't touch her."

"In other words, you're going to make it your personal mission to find every skeleton in her closet."

"Actually, I'm going to enlist the help of a dear family friend."

Until this very moment, I hadn't thought to approach Draco Jackson, a longtime Drakos family ally and my mentor. Draco and his heirs dominated the Nevada underworld with a reach going as far as the Northwest and south of the border, deep into Mexico. If anything happened in his territory, he'd know about it, especially the hidden activities of a rival's daughter.

My family's ties to Draco went back nearly seventy years. My great-grandfather, the original Christopher Drakos, had helped a barely eighteen-year-old Draco settle in the United States when his family in Japan ordered him to expand his family's reach into North America.

Draco was born into the *Ninkyō Dantai*, or more widely known as the Yakuza, the mafia that ruled the underworld of Japan. To this day, most of his extended family were still high-level members of one of the ruling clans in the organization.

"I hate to break it to you, but Draco has a soft spot for the Lykaioses."

"The same is true for myself. If he wasn't out of town this weekend, we'd be having dinner with him tonight."

"He raised Hagen Lykaios like a son, and he watches out for all of them."

"I know where Draco's loyalties lie. The man all but stepped in to replace Pappous after the crash. Hell, Draco seemed more vested in my success than I was, at times."

The one thing I could say about Draco was that he never, ever forgot his debts. Within hours of the confirmation of Pappous's death, two of his sons and three of his grandsons had arrived in New York with their men to join with the Drakos soldiers to ensure I stayed alive.

I'd known, the moment the news of the helicopter going down reached my ears, that the likelihood of an engine malfunction was less than zero.

Anyone who believed otherwise was either in on the assassination or condoned it.

Having Draco's backing essentially showed my uncle, his allies, and all of those who my grandfather had turned into rivals and enemies that even though I may have been only twenty-three when I'd taken over the family, I wasn't weak by any means and had the support to hold the Drakos territory.

I'd asked Draco why he'd dropped so much to support me, and he'd told me in his deep, Japanese-accented voice, "One never forgets those who gave him water when he was thirsty. Christopher had mercy on an eighteen-year-old idiot and helped me find a place in the world. I decided aiding his equally ill-prepared great-grandson was the least I could do."

I knew there was more to the story, but as with everything, Draco limited his explanations to basic truths and need-to-know information.

No matter what, I was eternally thankful to him.

Now I only hoped he or one of his many grandchildren had some information on the Ida's resident mob princess.

"From the way you spaced out into whatever plot you are concocting, it doesn't look as if anything I say is going to change your mind." Kasen headed in the direction of the giant array of glass doors leading to the hotel exit. "Like always, I'll be here to laugh my ass off and clean up your mess when the shit hits the fan."

I grabbed the door as he pushed through it, and we headed toward my waiting Spyder. "Dickhead. If it wasn't for me, you'd be an over-glorified errand boy."

"I *am* an over-glorified errand boy." Kasen's phone vibrated, and as he pulled it out of his pocket and read the display, the humor left his face and eyes.

"What's the problem?"

"How locked in is the Cypress port?"

"Solid. The contracts are signed and in the safe. All we have to do is execute the day we divide the trust and end the engagement. Why?"

"Tyler Mykos sent word Uncle Dearest and his equally fuckhead son just put in an offer to purchase it with an additional counteroffer of marriage to your fiancée."

A LITTLE AFTER ONE IN THE MORNING, I LOUNGED IN IDA'S Mesánychta Lounge, watching the hustle and bustle of Vegas nightlife mingle in and around the hotel. From my spot, I had a perfect vantage point of those entering and exiting the white marble hallways leading to the three high-end shows as well as the dark and dimly lit tunnel taking patrons into what was dubbed "The Underworld" leading to the five different nightclubs of the hotel.

One of them having the name Nyx, named after the goddess of night. I could only imagine what my beautiful fiery-tempered fiancée thought when she saw the sign of her namesake club for the first time. She more than likely rolled her eyes and walked right past it.

The Mykoses were turning out to be nothing as I expected. After the text from my temporary in-law, we set up a video conference where he relayed Albert and my cousin Hal's offer to replace me in his daughter's life as well as details on partnership with contacts in Central and South America.

Apparently, Phillip Mykos had taken Hal's counter marriage proposal as a personal insult. Mykos believed his word was a matter of honor and integrity. Everyone in our world understood how their family operated.

Albert was turning out to be a bigger pain in the ass than I thought.

What the fuck was his end goal? Neither he nor Hal had the support or manpower to run the family. And destabilizing the organization would only harm him in the long run.

Right now, I had other things on my mind. Like the fact I had to figure out my perfect fiancée's secrets. Kasen would do his research and get back to me.

Picking up my drink, I took a sip as a tall blonde walked past me and gave me a smile, but instead of keeping my focus on her, my attention shifted to a group coming from a private area of the hotel.

Was that who I thought it was?

No fucking way.

But it was.

Olympia Nyx Mykos, surrounded by at least ten men and women, moved in the direction of the Ida Underworld.

Gone was the fresh-faced, innocent-looking nature nymph in a casual, I-couldn't-care-less outfit. And in her place was this sultry vixen, wearing what look like an off-the-runway minidress, showing a body that made me want to punch every man who looked in her direction.

How the hell could she hide this side of herself from my men?

That was when a woman, dressed in casual linen pants and a cashmere sweater with an eerily similar appearance to Nyx, walked in her direction. They fist-bumped, exchanged a few words, and then passed.

A goddamned body double.

I was fucking right. Innocent, my ass. Now I'd find out what she was doing with all her time in Vegas.

Pushing to my feet, I threw a few bills on the table and made my way out of the lounge. As I neared her group, I heard an angry discussion and paused.

"I want another chance at a buy-in."

"There are no second chances. You know the rules."

"I'm not talking to you, bitch. I'm talking to your boss. She can speak for herself. She has a voice."

"Well, since you put it so nicely, David." I heard the slide of a blade. "I think I will use a few choice words with you."

A gasp sounded, and I shifted, completely in awe of what I was seeing. Nyx had the man named David pinned to the wall with what looked like some type of honed black blade pressed to his throat. Her people stood around her, blocking her from the view of the hotel guests and giving the appearance of a group of friends in an animated discussion.

The Mykoses had taught their sister and their people well.

No matter how good they were, they hadn't learned at the hands of Gio Drakos. I could maneuver in and out of crowds without detection long before most of Nyx's protection hit puberty. It would impress the hell out of me if even one of them sensed my presence.

Nyx leaned forward, giving the impression of a lover readying for a kiss. "Listen very carefully. Don't ever fuck with me or my business again. You knew the rules when you entered. You knew the buy-in. You knew the price you pay if you lost.

"I told you not to sit at that table. I told you that you were in over your head. I even offered to help you out of the hole you were digging after you lost the first hand and move you to a more manageable group. Did you listen? No. My kindness only goes so far. Don't play with money that doesn't belong to you."

"You think you're so tough. Does your family know what you do? Does your new fiancé? The right word in the right ears, and this all disappears."

Well, it looked as if the fucker knew about me. This was just getting more interesting by the second.

"David, it's not my throat you need to worry about, since it looks as if it's yours on the line at this very moment."

"Daddy and your brothers aren't here to clean up the mess for you, princess."

"Oh, but I don't need them to. You see, just like you stated, the right word in the right ear can make all of this disappear. Well, the same can be said of you. Remember the people in that room you played in? You fuck with me, you fuck with them. They don't like people threatening their business any more than I do."

Fear flashed on David's face.

"That's right. I would be scared if I were you."

"I'm sorry, Nyx. You don't understand the shit I'm in."

"And you thought threatening me would get you out of it. I trusted you, David. You tossed our friendship down the toilet."

"You can still trust me. I swear."

"Sure, I believe you." There was no hiding the sarcasm in her tone. "All you've shown me is to never go soft when it comes to vetting people. I won't make that mistake again."

"Come on, Nyx. Give me another chance. We've played in these games since we were kids."

"Answer this question. What would Tyler, Nico, Damon, or Evan do in my situation? They all grew up with you too. Pretend I was born with a dick instead of ovaries. Then think about this situation. Oh, wait. What would the Mykos Surgeon do? Papa's way of handling betrayal is pretty legendary."

The guy visibly paled.

"Exactly. Honor and integrity. It's a big deal to the Mykos Family. Did you know there is a room Papa likes to use for infractions against him? This way the mess is contained and easier to clean up. I have a key. Would you like to see the inside?"

"You wouldn't."

"I'll give you five choices on guessing who taught me how to use this knife." She traced the tip along David's jugular, and for some reason, that move got me as hard as if she'd just stroked my cock.

"What do you want me to do, Nyx?"

"I want you to leave Vegas and never, ever mention me or my games ever again. And that means the ones from back in the day too. One word, and you'll truly understand why they call me Silent Night."

"You're as fucked in the head as Tyler."

"Hooray, you guessed the right Mykos. Don't tell Papa or he'll get jealous. Papa thinks he's the only one allowed to teach me knife skills." She gave him a flirty smile that never quite reached her eyes. "Want to know a secret?"

"I...I'm afraid to ask."

"Tyler also taught me how to slice an artery so it causes the least amount of mess." She stepped closer to him, almost brushing her full body to his. "It took a lot of practice to get it just right. But then again, I was only thirteen when I learned so my hands weren't as steady back then. It took some practice, but now I'm as precise as a surgeon. Maybe one day they'll call *me* the Mykos Surgeon."

The look of utter horror on David's face was almost comical.

"Everything they say about you is true."

"Isn't there always a bit of truth to every rumor?" Nyx shrugged. "Maybe in my case, more than a bit. I'm just good at hiding it."

Her mindfuck game could rival the most seasoned in our world. Then again, the reputation the Mykos men carried ran along the lines of mind-annihilation so it would make sense the youngest of the group would pick up a thing or two.

Her face grew serious, and all traces of the bloodthirsty Mykos baby sister disappeared. "Do I have your agreement, David?"

"Fine."

"That doesn't sound like a yes to me."

"Yes. I'll keep my mouth shut."

"Good." She stepped back. "Oh, and don't even think about showing up to the engagement party."

"I don't have a choice."

"Make up something. Like when you told Janice you were in Boston with your father when you were actually in Miami fucking your mistress. If you can lie to your wife, I'm sure you can lie to your family."

Nyx gestured to a man near her, and he grabbed David, hauling him away.

Less than a few seconds later, Nyx sheathed the blade into its holder and handed it to a member of her detail. Closing her eyes, she leaned back against the wall where only moments earlier she had David pinned.

"You have that psycho Harley Quinn act perfect. The only thing missing is the blond hair with pink ends and your trusty bat," Stevie, the tall, striking woman dressed in a tailored suit observed as she settled next to Nyx.

After Stevie had caught my first interplay with Nyx in the garden, I'd learned as much as I could about Stevie Nem. The former model turned champion mixed martial artist, turned head of Nyx's security, had secrets of her own. However, since her secrets had no impact on my or Nyx's life, they'd remain buried.

"I prefer knives of all types," Nyx whispered as she pressed her fingers to her temple, and what looked like defeat flashed over her face. "All I wanted was just a night out to catch up with my bestie. Not this shit. First, it was the asshole I'm supposed to marry, and now this."

"This one is handled. You scared him enough to keep his mouth shut. I'm pretty sure he peed himself."

I couldn't help but smirk at that comment.

Nyx sighed. "At least those stupid lies everyone made up about me finally came in handy."

"That leaves the other asshole."

"Do you have to bring him up? I have enough on my plate

for one night."

"I don't get it. Why are you so salty about the fact he wants to sleep with you? It's not as if you aren't attracted to him. I'm the one who caught you eye-fucking each other in the gardens. I'm sure when you meet up with your bestie, she will agree with my summation."

"All you and Akari think about is sex, and for the record, I'm not going to just fuck anyone."

Who was this Akari person? Nothing from Kasen's reports mentioned anyone with that name.

"He's not just anyone. You're engaged to him, even if it's fake. Why not get a few dozen orgasms out of him while you're waiting out the year and change?"

I liked this woman. She was pleading my case for me.

"I'm not a whore."

"Who says you can't make him yours?"

That was a new one. Me being someone's whore.

"You definitely got into the same over-sugared fruit juices Akari likes. Neither of us is going to be anyone's whore because it isn't going to happen."

I may like this Akari too.

"You and this thing about finding the love of your life. Well, while you're looking for him, scratch an itch."

Her face reddened, and she looked around, glancing in the direction of her detail. "Seriously?"

Stevie folded her arms. "They are hired to only hear what we tell them to hear. Besides, it's not as if your protection isn't the first to know if you're fucking someone."

"You're so annoying. Why am I even listening to this?"

"I'm only stating the facts. You're way overdue. Maybe call

Akari's friend? I could have sworn you hit it off with that hottie."

"You mean the singer from Onyx Stone? No way. I'm too jealous of a personality to have women throwing themselves at my man all the time."

"I didn't say marry him. I suggested you fuck him."

"Okay. We need to change the subject. Let's go find Akari before you try to hook me up with some random guy walking by us since you think I have cobwebs in my cooch."

"You said it, not me."

"Asshole."

"No, that describes your fiancé. I'm your amazing and fabulous magic bodyguard."

"Come on. I want to drink and dance. Tomorrow, I plan to do nothing but vet every last motherfucker attending the game next week. I'm never going to let my history with anyone interfere with business again."

Nyx wearily set herself straight from the wall, adjusted her minuscule dress, and then stepped into the crowd with her entourage behind her.

I watched her disappear in the plethora of people, trying to process everything I'd just witnessed.

First, Olympia Nyx Mykos was a chameleon of the first tier, with the ability to play many roles. The evil, bloodthirsty mob princess sat right up there with the doe-eyed gardener I'd first set sights on.

Second, her ability with knives was laced in both truths and lies. Her reaction at the end conveyed how much she hated the role of bitch blade wielder but wouldn't hesitate to use it.

Third, the nature nymph had a dirty little secret she'd

engaged in from the time she lived in New York and had expanded her enterprise to Vegas.

And all arrows pointed to underground gambling.

Naughty, naughty.

My future bride was involved in something that could get her in a lot of trouble.

Was this what she meant when she said she wanted someone to accept all of her? No man in his right mind would let his woman take those kinds of risks. And I had no doubt, none of the Mykos clan had any clue of the activities of their precious princess.

Yes, I knew I was an ass, but the people Nyx tangled with in her games were undoubtedly worse than those her brothers or I dealt with regularly.

Now I had to find a way to catch her red-handed. Until I figured out the logistics of my plan, I might as well see how she burned off all the steam.

6

Nyx

"Pour me another. I need at least one more to take the edge off," I said to my bestie, Akari Ota.

She was the managing partner of Kato Kosmos, the newest of the nightclubs in the Ida. She'd arrived back into town earlier today after what we liked to call her quarterly required family time with her overbearing parents. And with the holidays steadily approaching, she would have no free time until after the New Year. Which meant she would have to visit them or have her family come to her. She'd chosen the lesser of the two evils.

Akari narrowed her black eyes, saying without words, "Girl, don't get me in trouble with your overprotective cousin," and then reached for the Firewater Reserve Whiskey tucked away on the top shelf behind her.

"Don't glare at me like that. If you had the night I did, you'd hand me the whole damn bottle."

She set two crystal tumblers in front of us, poured our drinks, and then pushed one toward me.

"Want to tell me what happened between the let's-hang-out-tonight call and our current state of *I want to kill my liver with this five-thousand-dollar bottle of spirits?*"

Picking up my drink, I took a healthy swallow and let the fiery liquid soothe my senses before replying with, "Assholes. That's what happened."

"As in the man-type of assholes?"

"Are there any other?"

"I feel like we missed a conversation or two during the week I spent in Seattle with my parents." She studied me as if I were an alien species. "When did you get a man? And why am I the last to know about it?"

I cringed. She was so going to let me have it. If there was anyone who would have my back in the situation I was currently in, it was Akari.

Both of us came from similar backgrounds. Our families were tied to shipping empires and the worlds of the syndicate, we were females in families full of males, and we'd moved to Las Vegas to get away from the rules and regulations we'd grown up using every means necessary to circumvent.

The main differences we had were our cultural backgrounds. Hers being Japanese and mine Greek, and that she'd grown up in Seattle and I was from New York.

She also happened to be the sister-in-law to Lana, Draco Jackson's granddaughter. Which gave her one extra point in the what-the-fuck-ometer, since I at least got away from having mob bosses up my ass all the time telling me what to do. Whereas, she constantly had an eye or two on her.

Who was I kidding?

I just happened to bribe the eyes on me with a cut of my business so they reported only the information I wanted to the powers that be.

"Do you remember when I mentioned I had a problem that I hoped to resolve by the time we met tonight?"

"I take it the man was the problem."

I took a deep breath. "You could say that. He's my fiancé."

"Your what?" She set her drink on the bar between us, grabbed the edge of the bar, and then leaned forward. "I need you to start at the beginning and don't leave a fucking thing out. If there is one thing I'm good at, it's knowing when you are lying, Mykos. That poker face of yours won't work on me."

I pressed my fingers to my temples for a brief moment, looked around to make sure only our protection stood near us, and then relayed the whole sordid Mykos-Drakos saga.

"So, let me get this straight. You're engaged to the head of a rival family, neither of you wants to marry the other, but he makes out big if you do get married. You offered him your portion of the trust to end the engagement, and he countered by saying he'd rather fuck you for the next year."

I nodded. "Yep. That about sums it up."

"Are you attracted to him?"

My thoughts shifted immediately to the insane way my body had reacted the instant my eyes connected with Simon's, the way my pulse had jumped, the way my nipples had beaded and my pussy had grown slick. Nothing like this had happened with any other man I'd ever met. I could still feel the sizzle of it deep down inside me.

Releasing a deep breath, I refocused on Akari and caught the knowing smirk on her face.

"Okay, then. You answered my question."

"Answered what question?"

"You want to fuck him."

I narrowed my gaze. "I'm not selling myself for my freedom."

"It's an exchange, not selling."

"I can't believe you right now."

"Nyx, this is all we've ever talked about. The chance to live a life away from what we grew up with. To have choices."

"Is this the way to do it?"

"Is it really that much of a hardship? The way you responded to my question says he's hot and you would totally bone him if he were anyone other than Simon Drakos. Tell me I'm wrong, and I'll call you a liar."

"You're so damn annoying."

"I just say it like it is. Besides, it's not as if you both aren't getting something out of it."

"I'm not whoring myself for my freedom."

"Think of it as you're mutually whoring yourselves. It's no different than two people hooking up randomly for a year and then parting ways. No emotions, just hot sex. The added benefit for both of you is that there is a healthy payout for your families, and you get to live your life here while he has his perfect debutante back home."

"I love how you justify an asshole blackmailing me into sleeping with him like this."

"Stop lying to yourself. I know you better than you think. The reason you're so mad is because he's the first man to pique your interest, and he happens to be the one who controls your future and your fortune."

I glared at her. "Let me repeat. You're so annoying. Why are we best friends, again?"

"Because I'm the only one who will put up with you and your multiple personalities." Akari picked up the decanter of whiskey and poured more into our tumblers. "Speaking of your many facets—is the goddess of night ready to handle her patrons next week, or are we canceling?"

"No, we can't cancel. There are way too many of our high rollers coming into town."

"Then I guess you'll have my usual spot saved for me."

"As long as you have the buy-in, your spot is assured."

"Can I ask you a question about your fiancé?"

Rolling my eyes, I answered with a, "Sure, why the hell not."

"Is he tall with a killer body, short black hair, a trim beard, and very green eyes?"

I stiffened as my grip on the tumbler in my hand tightened. "He's here?"

"I take that as a yes. He's coming through the crowd in our direction." Her gaze lingered behind me. "Okay. I give it to you. He's hot with a capital H. You definitely need to take him up on the offer."

"It's not an offer. It's blackmail."

"One that would have you losing your v-card with a hot-as-fuck guy."

"All you think about is sex."

She shrugged. "It's not as if you were saving yourself for

60

marriage. Given the chance, you'd have taken care of the deed long ago."

I couldn't deny the truth of her words. Growing up, all I ever wanted was to escape New York, so I spent all my energy focused on school. Then, when I wanted to date, a bunch of cockblockers—aka my brothers—and their men surrounded me whenever someone remotely interesting was in the vicinity.

After moving to Vegas, I had to learn to separate the authentic men from the ones looking for a good time. In the end, it had become too much work, and my clubs and garden management had taken over my life.

Damn. Thinking about the last few years, I really was boring as hell.

"Tell me I'm wrong," Akari probed, snapping me out of my thoughts.

Instead of answering her, I shot back my drink. "Tell me when he's here."

"Here," was the word spoken into my ear as a firm hand settled on the nape of my neck and then traced down my spine through the open back of my dress.

Goosebumps prickled my skin, and my breath immediately grew a bit shallow.

The smug amusement on Akari's face told me she'd let Simon get this close to me just to see my reaction to him.

Bitch.

"So, you must be the infamous asshole." Akari offered her hand to Simon.

"Among other things. I'm also Nyx's fiancé."

"I heard."

"And you are?"

"I'm the best friend. Akari Ota."

Simon studied her for a moment. "As in Travis Ota's baby sister?"

I couldn't help but smirk inside. He'd stepped in a pile of shit by saying that. Akari held a legendary name in the nightclub industry with her unique ideas and aesthetics. It was the reason Hagen had sought her out as a partner with this club. He wanted an edge on the competition no one else in Vegas had.

And thanks to my cousin's need to have the best working with him, I'd met the woman who turned out to be my kindred spirit and best friend.

Akari clenched her teeth. "As in Akari Ota, managing partner of Kato Kosmos and sixteen other establishments across the world."

"Now I can see why you're Nyx's friend. Similar personalities."

"Word of advice when dealing with women like Nyx and me."

"What is that?"

"Don't piss us off. Especially by thinking we want to be known by our family connections instead of as individuals. It makes some of us want to slice things off and others of us trigger happy."

"Good to know." His fingers curved around my exposed waist, making it almost impossible to breathe. "Is there a place my betrothed and I can speak in private? I have a response to her statement from earlier in the evening."

"My office. Nyx knows the way."

The idea of being in a room alone with him scared the shit

out of me. My body seemed to betray me at every turn, and who knew what would happen if we were behind a closed door.

Hell, already my libido hummed in anticipation.

Traitorous bitch.

"Let's talk, Nyx." The command in his voice had my throat drying up and a pulse of need shooting deep into my core.

"Who said I'm going anywhere with you? I'm in the middle of a night out with a girlfriend."

"I did. You have a hell of a lot more at stake in this than I do."

"Are you sure about that? In a year, you may end up with a wife you don't want. I say you have as much on the line as I do."

"That's where you're wrong. No matter what, I come out ahead. I'll remain the head of my family, have half of a giant trust, and most of all, I'll get to fuck you whenever I want. Whereas you'll lose this town, this life, this freedom you love so much."

I glanced to my side where Tony now had replaced Stevie to keep a watchful eye on us. He'd intervene within seconds of a signal from me. But it would only cause more problems for me.

Releasing a sigh, I shifted in my seat and whispered, "You could really make me hate you."

"I'm sure this won't be the last time you'll say that to me."

As I stood, I pushed his hold on my waist away, but he grabbed my wrist in a similar fashion to how he'd captured it in the restaurant, making my heartbeat accelerate.

His green gaze locked with mine. "Lead the way, Nyx."

"Stop."

"Stop what?" His lips curved at the corners, telling me he knew exactly what.

"Asshole."

Turning, I jerked my arm, but to no avail. I couldn't free my hand.

Moving around the bar, I shot Akari a glare. As my best friend, she'd been no help. Hell, she'd let him sneak up on me.

Akari mouthed, "Sorry. He's potent."

Yeah, wasn't that an understatement.

We remained quiet as I guided us through the dimly light hallways of Kato with its three levels of security. When we reached a large wooden door, I placed my palm on a security panel, waited for a beep, and then pushed open the door.

After we entered, I glowered at him. "You can let me go now. I'm not going to run. You have me captive in here."

"I had you captive out there too." He released my hand, stepped away from me, and leaned on the edge of Akari's glass desk.

Folding my arms across my body, I followed his stance and set my back against the closed door.

"You wanted to talk. Talk."

"You know it's inevitable between us."

"Keep dreaming."

"Tell me you don't feel it."

I stared into his hypnotizing emerald depths that seemed to pull me and lure this need I never realized lived inside me.

Licking my lips, I took in a slight breath, and then asked, "Feel what?"

"Exactly what's happening to you right now. I'm not even touching you, and the draw is killing you."

God, I hated him for what he was doing to me. I ached, especially between my legs.

"I can admit this attraction is unique. However, your sunny disposition tends to negate some of it."

"Liar. It turns you on."

"I don't sleep with men I've known less than a day."

"As I told you, sleeping is the last thing we are going to do."

"Let me rephrase my statement. I don't fuck men I've known less than a day."

"We have a year to get acquainted."

"The risks of anyone finding out are too much." I shook my head. "I won't let you trap me into a marriage. You get too much by marrying me. You admitted it yourself."

"You think sex is going to mean I will force you to the altar. Believe me when I say I'll stick to the bargain. I get plenty without the bonds of matrimony."

"Why should I trust you?"

"I never go back on my word. Besides, I've picked the woman I plan to marry, and you aren't her."

"Interesting. I find it hard to believe that she'll willingly wait it out while you fuck me out of your system."

"As far as she and everyone else is concerned, this is the real thing. If she's available at the end of this, I'll proceed with my plans. Otherwise, I'll select another candidate."

"It's all business with you, isn't it?"

"Life is business. Cleaner that way. Less complications."

"What if I change my mind and decide to marry you?"

"Then I guess I'll have a beautiful wife with a fetish for blades." He smirked. "But we know that won't happen. You've shown your cards already. You're desperate to keep this life you've built. You'll run before showing up at the altar."

I closed my eyes and dropped my head back against the door. I'd done exactly what he claimed.

Fuck. I'd played my hand too soon, instead of feeling him out.

Lifting my lids, I found him standing directly in front of me. When the hell had he moved, and why hadn't I noticed?

This man's presence wreaked havoc on my senses. Of all the people in the world to affect me this way, why was it him?

Getting involved with him spelled disaster on an epic level.

I had no experience in anything like this. Hell, I had no experience in anything. Much less a sex bargain.

"I'm not any man's whore."

He moved closer, his intoxicating scent of spiced cologne and soap teasing my senses. "You haven't been mine. You may like it."

"Not happening." I tilted my chin up, holding his stare and refusing to let this lure toward him overwhelm me, all the while knowing I was failing miserably.

"Tell me, Nyx," he crooned, a second before his palm closed over my throat, making me gasp and sending a spasming deep inside my core. "Would it really be so bad?"

His hold felt too good; the pressure made me crave things I shouldn't want with this man.

He ran his thumb over my lips, as a wave of desire flooded my cleft.

"Sex isn't supposed to be transactional." I grabbed hold of his muscled forearm and set my other hand on his chest to push him back, but instead, I curled my fingers into his shirt.

He tugged my neck to the side and ran his stubble along my jaw as he caged me with his body. "What else would you call it?

You want out of this marriage. I want to do every dirty, delicious thing imaginable to your body while giving you extraordinary pleasure. Agree and we both get what we want."

"It's never that simple."

His teeth grazed the shell of my ear, right before he bit, giving it a delicious sting, and it took all my strength not to whimper and beg for more.

"Of course, it is. No one besides us will know the details."

His words felt like a bucket of cold water thrown on me, and the haze of lust dimmed.

I pushed him away. "You mean besides the security and people who surround us day and night. I can't risk anything getting back to my family."

"You don't have much choice in this, Nyx. My offer is on the table until next week. Just know, only one way sets you free, but I get to fuck you no matter the outcome."

"You really are the asshole everyone calls you."

"I am everything Gio Drakos created."

7

SIMON

AROUND SIX P.M., FIVE DAYS AFTER MY ULTIMATUM TO NYX, I arrived outside the building housing Draco Jackson's private gentlemen's club on the outskirts of Las Vegas. I'd barely spent any time in New York, only flying in for a little over twenty-four hours before leaving to handle situations at hotspots in strategic port cities across the US.

Why, all of a sudden, we were having problems with organizational structure and compensation made no sense. Based on my advisers, we were too generous compared to others.

My gut said my fucker of an uncle had his hands elbow-deep in the chaos. Or should I say, his asshat son, my cousin, Hal.

I'd let them play their games. The fuckers had no idea the

Mykoses were in on my plans and were letting them believe they were open to the counteroffer they'd posed for the port and Nyx's hand.

Soon, I'd clean house and be rid of the trash. Right now, I had to pay my respects to the man whose territory I planned to visit regularly for the next year.

I'd barely stepped out of my SUV into the brisk early November chill when the doors to the nondescript building opened and four men dressed in immaculate black suits exited and waited.

As I approached, they all inclined their heads without saying anything.

When I moved into the entrance, a hostess approached me with a tray holding a warmed washcloth. I took the towel, wiped my hands, and placed it back on the holder.

"Follow me, sir," she instructed. "You are expected."

After working our way through the main area of a high-end gentlemen's club with dancers and servers preparing for a night of high-roller clients, we entered a private lounge where seven men of Japanese descent, ranging in age from midnineties to early thirties, were seated. They relaxed on a set of couches that no doubt cost well over fifty grand apiece.

In the center of the group sat Draco Jackson. His age-weathered face should have made him look frail and weak but had the opposite effect, giving him a honed, all-knowing vibe.

He owned the room and the people in it. Anyone who questioned it suffered at the pointed end of whatever cool, calculated discipline Draco decided to dole out for the disrespect.

As I approached, Draco's attention shifted from his

conversation to me. In less than a few seconds, he appraised me from head to shoes, taking in everything about me.

A light entered his dark gaze before he asked in Japanese, *"How did you enjoy your visit to my town last week?"*

The old mob boss never missed a beat when it came to what went down in his "town," as he like to call it.

If one viewed Vegas as a town, instead of the insanity of a city that it was.

"Hello, Oyabun," I responded in Japanese, giving him the formal welcome for a man at his level in the power structure in his organization and calling him "boss," before switching to English. "Las Vegas is interesting, as always."

He gestured to an empty seat near him. "What did you think of your fiancée?"

And why wouldn't his people know I'd made contact with Nyx?

"She isn't anything as I expected."

"Of course, she isn't. None of the Mykoses are as they appear. You should remember this."

I took my place on the sofa and picked up the scotch one of the servers set in front of me. "You could have warned me her best friend was your grandson-in-law's sister."

"Just as you could have told me you were going to visit my territory to interfere in a deal that could cause you endless grief." He tilted his tumbler in my direction in a gesture of welcome before taking a sip, and I followed suit.

"I wanted to set ground rules for our engagement."

"I'm sure that went well," Sota, the eldest of Draco's grandsons, mused with a smirk. "At least you survived without having your throat slit."

Fucker.

We'd grown up together and communicated almost weekly, if not more. The least he could have done was give me a heads-up about Nyx. But then again, if he was told to keep it quiet, he'd follow orders.

Sota and his brothers had taken over most of the Jackson operation, controlling Vegas and the western United States, from his father, Kota, Draco's oldest son.

Though, no one would ever question that Draco still led the Jackson clan. He may have retired from the day-to-day workings of his organization long ago, but nothing happened without his knowledge.

I envied the closeness of the Jackson family. They worked like a well-oiled machine. Everyone knew their role and understood the importance of expanding the empire. Jealousy seemed nonexistent. In fact, the thought of sitting on one's ass and collecting on the family's reputation was simply inconceivable to any of them.

"So, you know about her? Why am I not surprised? The Jacksons keep tabs on everyone in Vegas."

"What have you discovered, Simon?" Draco asked, without confirming anything.

"All the rumors about her are laced in truth, especially the hellion part. Away from New York, she acts like she's pure as sunshine, but she isn't anywhere close to that. It's all an act."

"I wouldn't assume too much about her. A chameleon only performs to fit the role. It would do you good to accept who she is when she believes no one is watching."

"Are you saying she is a sweet victim of gossip who just happens to like throwing knives as a hobby?"

"Just as we know no matter how hard Gio tried to make you into his image, you are still very much Kyros's son."

I showed no outward reaction to the dig at Pappous. One thing Draco never shied away from was conveying his disagreement with the way Pappous handled his relationships with his sons, especially my father.

To Draco, family was everything, and Gio Drakos had destroyed his, due to his pride and greed.

I wouldn't disagree with Draco's sentiment. However, Pappous taught me one valuable lesson with the death of my parents.

To keep the family running, one could never have any weaknesses.

"No disrespect, *Oyabun*. Olympia Nyx Mykos is no innocent. She's duped you as she has done with everyone else around her. She has an end goal, and I stand in her way, which pisses her off."

"I believe it is the other way around. You're frustrated that you've met a woman who won't put up with your way of doing business. Gio's methods won't work on her. A wise man would remember women are shrewd opponents."

"She wants out of this marriage. I gave her an option."

"There is no out for either of you." The finality of Draco's statement grated against my nerves. "The clause only works if you don't touch her."

"That is not what the clause says. I know it inside and out."

"You will not touch her and walk away, Simon." The order in Draco's voice had my temper flaring.

Of all the people I dealt with daily, I expected Draco to have my back in all things. His warning me away from Nyx felt like a punch to the gut.

"Why are you protective of her? Is it her relationship to the Lykaioses, her friendship with your in-law, or something personal?"

"Let's say it is all of the above. She has a place in my circle just as you do."

"Meaning?"

Draco lifted a bushy white brow, telling me I'd overstepped. "There are things I keep for my own benefit. You know how this game works. What I will tell you is that I won't work against you. Trust the process."

What the fuck could he mean by that?

"The process involves my marrying the Mykos Hellion?"

"Exactly."

"Respectfully, I disagree."

"Is that right? Explain to me how you plan to avoid this marriage that took over a hundred years to come to fruition."

"Neither of us are suited. We have different visions for our future."

Hell, even her family agreed and offered me a fucking port to back out of our engagement. Though, I couldn't say any of this to Draco, since the terms of my agreement with the Mykoses remained between us.

Draco remained quiet for a few moments, a line forming between his brows. "Are you saying this meeting with her was business? Is that what you are telling me?"

He knew damn well it wasn't.

"I'm not going to lie—my fiancée is beyond attractive. However, just because I want us to stay entertained for the next year doesn't mean I want to tie myself to her for the rest of my life."

The hardening of his jaw told me he found my response lacking, and I'd essentially pissed him off.

Well, fuck. This wasn't turning out anything like I expected.

"And has she agreed to your choice of entertainment?"

Keeping my tone emotionless, I responded with, "We're working out the terms."

"She isn't the naive girl the world believes, Simon. You'll get more than you can chew if you don't watch how you play your cards with her."

I studied Draco.

The annoyance had shifted in his black irises to a calculating glint, something I had no doubt he planned to keep to himself.

And his comment about her being part of his circle meant they shared some affection between them.

"Cards? Are you saying she's a card shark?"

"She's definitely that. Don't play against her unless you plan to lose."

"I'm less likely to lose if I go in with the odds heavily in my favor."

"You have more to lose than you realize." Draco lifted his tumbler to his lips, took a healthy gulp, and shook his head. "I'm going to enjoy this."

"Enjoy what?"

"Watching you crumple at the feet of the goddess of night."

"I'm called the master of darkness. Darkness conquers the night."

"Wrong. You need to brush up on your mythology. Nothing

conquers the night. Darkness is a companion of the night as long as she allows it."

It took all of my strength not to roll my eyes. Was I actually receiving an ancient Greek mythology lesson from a Yakuza mob boss?

"That's all I'm asking of her, an agreement on how to handle our engagement for the next year."

"It looks as if you are going to proceed with your plan no matter the advice I send your way." He pursed his lips and sighed. "You know where to find me when things fall apart."

"What, exactly, do you think is going to happen to me?"

"The same thing that happened to me." He held my gaze, something like resignation flashing in his irises.

"And that was?"

"If I told you, you'd change the outcome. I think I'll keep it to myself. This is a lesson you have to learn, my boy. For me, it worked out. You may not be so lucky."

A LITTLE BEFORE ELEVEN IN THE EVENING, I STEPPED OUT ONTO the balcony of my suite at a hotel owned by one of the Lykaios rivals and stared down at the Vegas Strip forty-two stories below. From my vantage point, Las Vegas Boulevard seemed like a world away, with its pedestrians and vehicles lit by the glow of the streetlights and the multitude of illuminated signs.

I could admit this resort couldn't hold a candle to any of the Lykaios properties, from the view to the amenities. However, if I wanted to remain under the radar of the watchful gazes of

Nyx's cousins and ultimately, her brothers, I had no choice but to stay in alternative accommodations.

The visit with Draco was anything but typical. It felt cryptic and left an unsettled lump in the base of my stomach. Then again, no other man besides Pappous possessed the ability to crawl into my head and plant seeds of doubt in myself or my plans.

What was it about Nyx Mykos that made everyone so ready to step between her and the world?

It was obvious he viewed her in a grandfatherly way. Maybe this led to his protectiveness toward her and this need to warn me about her. No, the look in Draco's eyes said he expected things to blow up in my face.

What could go wrong with this situation with Nyx besides her family finding out we slept together?

My phone buzzed in my pocket. Pulling it out, I read the incoming text on the display.

NYX: *Hey Asshole,*

Here is an answer to your proposal.

Fuck off.

My brothers told me all about your deal. You're a piece of work.

It will be a cold day in hell before I sleep with you.

You want the damn port, then you play by my rules.

And if you didn't get it the first time:

Fuck off.

As if she'd known the exact way to erase any of the uneasiness Draco had woven into my head, I smiled.

ME: *Are you sure that is the tactic you want to take with me?*

NYX: *What other tactic is there? You're lucky I kept your proposal to myself instead of telling my brothers.*

ME: *I'm curious. Why didn't you tell your brothers? Are you afraid I found out something about you when I was in Vegas?*

NYX: *You know nothing about me, Simon Drakos.*

ME: *I know that the next time I see you, we're going to end the night with you coming around my cock.*

Yeah, I was an ass for being so crude, but something about this woman made me want to push all her buttons.

NYX: *Put your cock anywhere near me, and I'll cut it off.*

ME: *That's a lie, and you know it. Especially since we both know I can make you wet with a look.*

NYX: *I really hate you.*

ME: *Doesn't change the fact it's true.*

NYX: *Don't even think about showing up in Vegas again as you threatened last week. I'll make your life difficult.*

ME: *What makes you believe that I'm not already in your precious city?*

NYX: *Then I suggest you get on your fancy jet and return to your debutante.*

ME: *But I'd rather stay here and spar with you.*

NYX: *I mean it. Come one step near me, and I will make you regret it.*

ME: *I expect nothing less from the goddess of night.*

NYX: *Asshole.*

I lifted my attention to Kasen as he opened the glass door separating the balcony and the penthouse.

The look on his face said he had information I needed to hear. Moving in his direction, I slid my phone into my pocket. I could wait a few minutes to antagonize Nyx some more.

"You aren't going to believe what I just found out." Kasen shook his head. "You were fucking right about everything."

77

"Want to elaborate? I'm right about a lot of things."

"Dickhead," Kasen muttered. "Your future bride."

"Meaning?"

"She's involved in the underground gambling circuit up to her eyeballs."

"How did you discover this?"

Kasen handed me an envelope. "This was delivered courtesy of Sota."

I lifted the flap and pulled out a card with a note attached to the top.

This stays between us. What you do with the information is up to you. I owe you for keeping quiet about your fiancée. I would have told you if my hands weren't tied. Remember, all consequences are on your neck.

Pulling off the note, I studied the information on the cardstock. It detailed a location, coincidently a suite in one of the private towers of the very hotel I was staying in, a time, a code to a specific elevator, and the number twenty-nine million.

"What do you plan to do?" Kasen asked.

I smiled. "I'm planning to play some poker."

8

NYX

"YOU'RE GOING TO MAKE A KILLING."

I shifted my attention to Stevie as she positioned herself at
my side.

"That we are." Smiling, I leaned against a wall in a hidden
corner of one of the two palatial sky suites in the Las Vegas
Grand Palace Casino and Resort.

This was the perfect vantage point to enjoy a prime view of
tonight's games and some of the wealthiest individuals in the
world playing high-stakes poker. The people at the tables
ranged from royals of various houses around the world to
movie stars, industrialists, billionaires, and anything in
between.

After the shit from last week, I'd gone above and beyond to
vet those who garnered an invitation tonight, making sure to

learn anything and everything about each person. Maybe calling in some of my friends with connections that would probably make every hair on my dear father's and brothers' heads gray within seconds was going a bit far, but I wasn't going to take any chances.

Never would I let a personal relationship color my view on people again. Business was business.

Wasn't that how my asshole fiancé had put it?

Every one of these individuals could visit the VIP high-roller rooms in the many casinos in the city; however, none of them could broker the type of secondary deals taking place at my tables.

I wasn't talking about the pots ranging from a few hundred thousand to tens of millions, where I took a percentage cut, but the ones made between the hands of cards or over cocktails and small talk.

My events provided the opportunity for people who could never meet in public to conduct business or engage in other ventures.

If caught, every one of us could land in hot water, but not a single soul would utter a word. Too much was at stake for all of us. Reputations, political futures, inheritances, and the biggest one of all—federal and international prosecution.

"Once everyone settles at the end of the night"—Stevie handed me a cocktail—"I suggest we close shop for at least a month or so. Things are too hot right now, especially with your fiancé intent on getting in your pants."

Taking the martini, I sipped the potent concoction and hummed.

Akari sat at a table across the room with a cold glint in her dark eyes.

She'd wait until the stakes rose a few hundred thousand higher before she went in for the kill. After all the times she'd attended one of my events, the men at her table couldn't get past her looks and her family connections, always underestimating her cunning. That was until she cleaned them out.

More power to her.

I waited until Akari won the hand to say, "Simon can go to hell, for all I care. He thought he could trick me into sleeping with him. Fuck him. I'm not worried. He wants that port, then he'll leave me the hell alone."

I still couldn't believe the nerve of him, trying to trick me. Fucker.

And then not having anything better to say in the text than to tell me he planned to sleep with me the next time he saw me.

Asshole.

"Tony agrees with me. It's better for you to play the feisty horticulturist who loves knives for the time being. Silent Night needs to take a break. This double life of yours is going to get you in trouble."

"I won't live in fear. Simon Christopher Drakos has no power over me."

"You can lie to yourself all you want, but we all know the truth. If he catches one whiff of this, it doesn't matter what deal he set with your family. He has all the ammunition he needs to enact the morality clause for the contract."

"Archaic, double-standard bullshit is what it is." I folded my arms across my body, feeling the urge to punch Simon just for existing.

"I'm the last person to disagree with that sentiment. However, it doesn't change the fact the clause is part of the contract between the families. You cannot engage in anything questionable. And this is not only questionable but as illegal as it gets."

"Outside of sleeping with him, do you have any suggestions on handling this issue?"

"Nothing comes to mind. Let's hope your secret stays safe for at least one more night."

"From your lips to God's ears."

At that moment, my phone buzzed with an incoming text. Glancing down, I growled.

SIMON: *I discovered a secret, Goddess. Want to know it?*

"Who is it?" Stevie asked.

"Apparently God isn't listening to my prayers tonight."

"Meaning?"

I showed Stevie the message, and she laughed. "Are you going to bite? For someone with his reputation, he seems to have a playful side. Well with you, anyway."

Ignoring her, I typed in my response.

ME: *I couldn't care less. As long as you stay in New York, you can do as you please.*

Almost immediately, he replied.

SIMON: *What makes you think I'm in New York? I did imply I'd returned to Vegas during our previous chat.*

A shiver coursed down my spine.

ME: *Let me rephrase: as long as you stay away from me, I don't care.*

SIMON: *Goddess, why would I stay away from you? You're my fiancée. I have a vested interest in you.*

ME: *Whatever. I'm busy. Find someone else to bother.*

SIMON: *Too busy to discuss the secret I discovered?*

ME: *I don't care.*

SIMON: *If that's how you want to play it. I think you should go answer your door.*

The penthouse elevator doorbell rang, making me freeze.

I glanced at Stevie. "I thought Draco declined the invitation."

"He did." Stevie gestured with her head to the security team, and they moved into position along the hallway leading to the front entrance of the suite.

Stevie and I moved to the bar area where we kept the monitors with the feed to view the elevators.

Staring directly at the camera was Simon. As if he had no doubt I was the one watching him at the moment.

He'd come alone.

Another indication he had no fear of the outcome of this night.

Continuing to look at the camera, he typed on his phone and another message pinged on my phone.

SIMON: *How about a private game, Goddess?*

My heartbeat roared into my ears, and a lightheadedness prickled at the back of my mind.

His lips curved at the corners, giving the camera one last smirk right before he moved to the keypad. He punched in a code, and the lift doors opened.

"You don't think Draco would have given him the information, do you?" Stevie asked as she set a hand on my shoulder.

"No, he'd never betray me."

My relationship with Akari and Draco's granddaughter, Lana, made me an honorary family member, but I'd also helped Draco on a personal project requiring my horticultural skills.

Which could only mean it had to be one of his grandsons. I bet it was Sota.

He still hadn't gotten over the fact I'd refused to give him his Viper back after he lost it in one of our monthly poker games.

It wasn't my fault he got cocky and bet the damn thing.

"You'll handle this," Stevie tried to reassure me, but we knew no matter how well-meaning her intentions, it was all bullshit.

The elevator doors opened into the penthouse, and I felt all the breath leave my lungs.

A shiver ran down my spine as I heard the deep timbre of his voice say, "I'm here to see my lovely fiancée. I'm sure she won't mind me observing."

"Let him pass," Stevie whispered into her wrist mic.

A few seconds later, Simon came around the corner.

Dear God. Did he have to look so good?

The black custom-tailored suit accentuated his well-honed body, and the open collar of his shirt gave the slightest hint of the tattoos etched on his skin. He oozed this aura of restrained danger I shouldn't find so alluring.

My fingers clenched the phone in my hand as his attention fixed on me.

"Got you," he mouthed.

"What did you say about him having no power over you?"

I stared into his green eyes, feeling as if he held my world in a vise grip. No, that wasn't it. He controlled it.

Instead of answering Stevie, I stood transfixed as Simon

came toward me. The feral gleam in his gaze told me he had me exactly where he wanted me. His captive at his mercy.

A low pulse of need began to throb between my legs, and my nipples beaded.

I wasn't sure whether I wanted to run or hold my ground. Either way, one thing held true, I wouldn't come out of this unscathed.

He stopped a mere foot away from me, uncaring of the number of people vested in who he was and what he was doing in the room.

Taking the mobile from my hand, he tucked it into his jacket pocket. "You're mine, Goddess."

Goosebumps prickled my skin. "Why do you keep calling me goddess?"

"Nyx is the goddess of night." He cupped my face and then ran his thumb over my lips. "And you run the Silent Night."

"And what does that make you?"

He leaned forward as if he were going to kiss me but stopped when he was a hairsbreadth from me.

His pupils grew not colder, but calculating. "What do they call me in our world? I find it appropriate in our case."

My breath grew shallow.

"I'm your Master of Fortune and Darkness."

"You think the darkness controls the night."

"This darkness does. It controls her fortune too."

"Simon, please don't."

"Don't what? Make you come for the next year or push the morality clause?"

Before I could respond, Akari moved behind us. "I see you've crashed our private soirée."

"Looks that way."

"I suggest the two of you hold the conversation about popping cherries and the next year over a private game at the end of the evening. You're drawing attention."

Simon's hold on my face tightened for a fraction of a second while he continued to stare into my eyes, and for the first time since I met Akari, I truly wanted to strangle her.

"I believe that is a perfect idea, Ms. Ota," he said as he traced his thumb over my lower lip. "I also appreciate the additional information on my bride."

"Have you lost interest?" I asked. "Don't men like you want experienced women?"

"Not in the least. It only means I don't have to erase anyone from your memory, and I get to teach you everything you'll ever need to know." He stepped back, the loss of his touch leaving a coldness on my skin. "I'll remain by the bar and watch how the mistress of Silent Night operates. See you at the end of the night, Goddess."

Clenching my teeth, I grabbed hold of Akari's wrist and yanked her in the direction of my banker, Natty.

"What the fuck? Was it necessary to throw that in there?"

"I was trying to help. I thought it would scare him off."

Stopping a few steps before we reached Natty, I glared at Akari. "Obviously, your plan backfired."

"It was worth a shot." She shrugged. "At least, it's out there now. Not like you would have shared it with him voluntarily."

"You don't know this."

She rolled her eyes and then muttered, "Bullshit."

"I'm going to ignore you now. I have work to do." Turning to

Natty, I waited for her to hand me her customary account of the totals currently in play at the tables.

"The take's better than we could have expected." Natty passed me a red envelope.

Opening the flap, I pulled out the paper and read the number.

Sixty-nine-point-three million, without the inclusion of the buy-ins.

Well, okay then.

Simon definitely was about to get a prime view of how I operated.

Glancing in his direction, my breath hitched.

He leaned an elbow on the bar top and held a tumbler of red-tinged liquid, Penny's special reserve Firewater I'd stocked for tonight.

He'd taken off his suit jacket, throwing it over the back of his chair, and rolled up his shirtsleeves, revealing the tattoos on his arms as well as the defined muscles that disclosed he wasn't a man who sat behind a desk but one who used his hands more often than not.

And those hands of his.

How the hell was I attracted to his hands? Maybe it was the strength in them as he'd held my wrists.

This man had my mind a twisted mess, and now I was in a fuck-ton of trouble.

He studied me as a predator stalked his prey. It was as if he wanted me to have a false sense of safety, all the while knowing there was nowhere to escape.

Anyone who glanced in his direction would know he'd

staked his claim on me. And for some insane reason, it aroused me.

Dear God. Did he have to look at me like that?

"Who is he?" Natty asked. "I've never seen a man twist you up like this."

"Her asshole fiancé," Akari answered for me.

She coughed. "Her what?"

"You heard right." Akari moved in next to me. "Our girl is engaged."

"Wait." Natty set a hand on my arm, but I kept my gaze on Simon's. "Less than a month ago, you were complaining about needing a man who you couldn't scare away. And now you're getting married. That was fast."

"That's the understatement of the year," Akari added.

Simon lifted the tumbler to his lips and then swallowed the spirit down before cocking a brow in challenge.

Fucker was in a stare-off with me.

He wanted me to look away.

And why the hell did I find this so fucking hot? I was seriously demented.

"Well, I guess you got what you asked for."

"Meaning?" I asked, knowing I had to jump into the conversation or Akari would keep adding in her two cents.

Simon set his glass on the bar top without shifting his gaze from mine. Something in his dark green irises had my pulse jumping. It felt almost as if he was readying to pounce at any moment.

"This isn't one you can scare. In fact, he may be the type to give as good as he gets. Maybe even more."

Natty's words felt like a bucket of cold water on my libido, drawing my focus to her and breaking my concentration on Simon.

Shit. Fucker won. Like everything else tonight.

Releasing a deep breath, I stated, "I think we should pay attention to our guests and not my personal life."

"I guess I touched a nerve." The humor in her tone told me she'd caught the interaction between Simon and me. "For the record, the sparks flying between the two of you from the moment he walked in could have lit the room on fire."

"I couldn't agree with you more, Natty."

I glared at Akari. "Why are we best friends?"

"Because no one else will put up with your ass."

9

SIMON

A VIRGIN.

At first, I wasn't sure I'd inferred Akari Ota's words correctly. Then, when Nyx confirmed them with her dig about losing interest, I felt as if she'd punched me in the gut.

In this day and age, how the fuck had she stayed without a lover into her midtwenties? Then again, she had four overprotective brothers and a father known as the Mykos Surgeon. If that wasn't a deterrent, I wasn't sure what was.

Even when I was a virgin, the thought of being with one had never crossed my mind. Hell, my first time was with the college-aged sister of one of my guards who wanted to "train" the Drakos heir for the future.

Now, here I sat, seriously planning to do this.

I swirled the amber liquid in my tumbler.

A better man would stop right now. A better man would give her the freedom she craved and let her find this ideal future husband. Then again, no one would ever mistake me for even a decent man, much less a better one.

Gio Drakos's bastard replica, yes.

A good man, no.

Something about Nyx Mykos drew me to her, and the thought of not touching her seemed inconceivable.

There was no choice for either of us. For the next year, I had to let it play out.

Maybe it was the way she constantly challenged me or told me to fuck off. Her temper turned me on instead of pissing me off as it would have with anyone else.

Hell, why the fuck was I questioning it? I held the cards in this game. I deserved a little enjoyment with all this bullshit I handled every day.

Nyx shifted her long black hair over one shoulder as she leaned down to whisper something into the ear of an elderly woman decked out in jewels worth as much as the money played at four of the tables near her.

The way Nyx worked the room showed a knowledge of everyone's likes, dislikes, nuances, and mood.

Many of the players came from backgrounds bound to cause any one of the Mykoses, if not all of them, a heart attack or two.

The fact she seemed to have some of the most dangerous people in the world charmed as if they were long-lost friends was a feat in itself.

For a split second, I wondered what it would be like to have a woman with Nyx's skills by my side. She'd know how to handle everyone around her. No one would ever mistake her for a wallflower or a delicate prize to show off.

No, I couldn't let my thoughts go in that direction. A Mykos would bring nothing but chaos to my existence. A calm woman who knew her place in my life was the right choice. None of this hellion shit.

At that moment, I heard a thick Russian-accented voice bellow, "Nyx, please tell me it's not true. You told me that you had no time for relationships, and now I hear you're engaged."

A pang of irritation hit, and I searched the room for Nyx. I found her by a group of men and women who congregated near a high-top table. Among the group were a few members of various syndicate families throughout Asia.

The one who'd just spoken looked near sixty and sported a wedding band. I realized he was Petre Ivanov, the head of an oil manufacturing conglomerate based out of Moscow. Though everyone knew it was true, no one would ever openly state he also led one of the largest and well-funded Bratva organizations in Russia.

Yes, Tyler Mykos would definitely lose his shit if he ever learned his baby sister engaged in small talk with a man with a reputation for drinking the blood of his enemies.

Literally.

I'd done some fucked-up shit, but I drew the line at ingesting my enemies.

And the fact Nyx seemed to have him wrapped around her little finger truly was a sight to see.

And what the hell was wrong with me that I was actually turned on by this?

This woman was making me lose my mind.

"Well, I was holding out hope for you, but since you're taken, I settled for someone else." Nyx lifted her lashes and met my scowl with a smirk.

"*Malaya moya*, come walk with me for a moment. I want to ask you something in private," the old man spoke in what I assumed was his version of a whisper but loud enough for everyone around him to understand to get lost.

As if on cue, people shifted, but with finesse, Nyx tucked her arm into his and then guided him away from the group. He, in turn, maneuvered her in my direction.

The old man wanted me to hear his conversation. My guess stood firmly in the "warn me away from Nyx" camp, like everyone else today.

"Did something happen that worries you tonight, Petre?"

"No. It is you I'm concerned about. I hear things."

"What did you hear?"

"I've been around a long time, *Zaychik*. I know how families like ours work. If this marriage isn't something you want, give me one word, and I will stop it. Drakos does not scare me."

Nyx's back went ramrod straight, and I had no doubt she wanted to glance over her shoulder in my direction.

"His presence here should give you all the answers you need."

"Then he accepts who you are and what you do?"

"As well as any man in his circumstance can."

"Then I trust you will come to me if things change in your situation. While Jackson plays matchmaker, know that I've picked a side. In fact, my family chose their side when my uncle Victor took Julia from the original Drakos."

Well, fuck.

This cleared up who helped the first Mykos heiress and her lover hide from everyone. As a member of the Bratva, he could have disappeared, and no one would have been the wiser. There was no way the Mykoses couldn't have known about the connection.

Could they have helped her escape the marriage and made it seem as if she ran?

Nyx coughed and set a hand on Ivanov's forearm. "Say that again."

"Come now. You have to know things from the past aren't always as they are presented."

"I'm not following."

At least, Nyx's confusion revealed she knew nothing of her family's history if what Ivanov was implying was true.

"In a family where daughters and sisters are rare, fathers and brothers will go to extraordinary lengths to protect them. Especially when it comes to tying that daughter to a family with a reputation for their cruelty and love of the bottom line."

Ivanov's words transported me back in time to one of the many lectures Pappous gave me about how he'd failed somewhere along the line and raised weak Drakos men who knew nothing about ruling in the way of the family predecessors and how he'd make sure he'd correct his mistake with me.

"Are you saying everything I've believed since I was born is a lie?"

"That is for you to decide. Though I don't suggest you ask your family, or you may have to divulge who shared the information, and that could lead to other questions. Wouldn't you agree?"

She sighed and then nodded as if accepting the truth of Ivanov's words.

"Does this mean that, since my great-aunt was also your aunt, in some very Greek way, we are family?"

"In a very Russian way, you are family. And I watch out for my own." His tone brooked no argument, going from lighthearted to commanding and fatherly.

"Is that why you wanted Simon to hear this entire conversation? You're watching out for me? Making sure I don't get into too much trouble?"

I wanted to laugh at her sheer ballsiness. The woman pulled no punches.

Ivanov's face softened, and a slight smile touched his lips. "Since you keep so much from your brothers and father, I feel it's my duty to make sure those around you know that you have connections in high places."

"Spasiba." Nyx leaned up, kissing Ivanov's cheek. "You don't need to worry about me. I'm going to be okay."

"For your sake, I hope you are right." Ivanov shot a warning glance in my direction. "I sure hope you are right."

———

AROUND THREE THIRTY IN THE MORNING, ALL OF THE PLAYERS, including Akari, were long gone from the penthouse. A cleaning crew like none I'd ever seen before worked to make the five-thousand-square-foot suite look as it had prior to the night's event. They moved as if in a well-choreographed

dance around each other, knowing every one of Nyx's
expectations and requirements. They also dressed in the
clothing of other hotel guests and not in that of a
housekeeping team.

Nyx stood across the room from me, engrossed in a
conversation with her security lead and banker. Just a few
moments earlier, they'd exited the primary bedroom after
finalizing the accounting of the evening's take.

Something I had no doubt lay around a quarter of the total
value of the trust she'd inherit at the conclusion of our
engagement.

No wonder she'd offered it to me. She had no use for any of
it if tonight was any indicator of the type of profit she netted
each time she held a Silent Night event.

Which had me wondering how much my fiancée was
actually worth. And why the hell was she digging in the dirt all
day and working a regular job when she could spend her days
relaxing and enjoying her life?

The woman confused the hell out of me.

As if sensing my thoughts, her gaze lifted to mine for a brief
second before she returned her attention to the group in front
of her. A slight tinge of heat colored her cheeks, telling me she
felt the time ticking away until we were alone and we
conducted our private discussion.

No matter how much she may want to deny it, we were
going to happen whether I'd found out her secret or not. This
attraction was too visceral.

Eventually, we would have found ourselves in a situation
where we'd end up fucking each other raw.

Though, knowing what I did about her, I'd have to take it

slower, seduce her into it. Make it so she compared any man she took to bed in the future to me.

However, at the moment, the idea of her being in anyone else's bed made me want to punch something.

Deciding I'd spent enough time waiting, I stood and moved in Nyx's direction.

Her onyx eyes locked with mine, a mix of wariness, and if I wasn't mistaken, curiosity. The people around her moved away to finish up whatever they were doing.

"How long until our private game?" I asked as I approached.

She licked her lips, her breath growing unsteady. "I wasn't sure if you were serious."

"I'm always serious about poker. I rarely lose."

"I can say the same for myself. However, those games aren't fixed."

"Are you forfeiting before a card is even dealt?"

Fire lit her gaze. "Not a chance. I'll set up a game on the dinner table."

"Good." Reaching up, I ran a thumb over her full lower lip. "When will everyone leave?"

She swallowed as her pupils dilated. "In about five minutes. Stevie and the team are doing a final sweep of the penthouse, then they will head out, locking all access to the suite, including the elevator."

"I thought you'd try to run."

She lifted her chin as a crease formed between her brows. "I don't run from anything."

"You may change your mind."

"And I don't scare easily."

"We'll see."

"Yes, we will." She turned, but I grabbed hold of her wrist.

"Ivanov gave you an out. Why didn't you take it?"

She gave me a calculating smile that had me wanting to show her what she could do with that luscious mouth of hers. "He wanted you to hear the conversation."

"He isn't known for wasting his words. There is a purpose for everything he does. He waited to tell you the truth about the past and within my earshot for a reason."

"Yes, to scare you."

"I believe I've established I don't scare easily, as well. In fact, I'm more intrigued than ever." I slid my hand from her wrist, up her elbow, over her shoulder, and then cupped the back of her neck.

The sharp inhale of her breath and the goosebumps prickling her skin gave me a sense of triumph in this battle of wills we seemed to have started.

"You didn't answer my question, Nyx."

"You mean about Petre?" Her palm settled on my chest.

"Yes."

"It's simple—I don't hide behind other people when it comes to my challenges. Not my father, or my brothers, not anyone."

"I'm a challenge?" I leaned forward, grazing my teeth across her bottom lip and watching her lashes flutter closed for a second.

"Most definitely," she responded in a husky whisper.

A throat cleared behind us, making Nyx immediately pull away from me. Her face flushed from arousal and embarrassment.

"We will lock up and leave the two of you to your…private game," Nyx's security lead stated, giving both of us a smirk.

"Thank you." Nyx followed her team to the elevator, speaking in low tones with Stevie.

A few minutes later, Nyx returned, apprehension etched all over her face.

"Ready to deal, Ms. Mykos?"

10

NYX

MY HEARTBEAT POUNDED IN MY EARS AS WE STARED AT EACH other from across the room.

No matter what hand I played tonight, the outcome remained the same.

I lost.

Hell, the game had started and ended the moment he stared at the camera and punched the code for the elevator doors.

Everything that had happened since then was him playing with me, watching my tells, raising the stakes, toying with me.

It was mind-fucking at its best.

He'd had me where he wanted me from the moment I saw him in the botanical gardens on my knees.

The fact I was more aroused than I'd ever been in my life pissed me off to holy hell.

Of all the men in the world, why would the gods decide it was this one to pull this kind of reaction from me?

Trust me to find a jackass attractive.

Every little touch drew me, every look, every interaction, as if he wanted me to crave him, need him.

Asshole.

"Nothing to say, Nyx?"

"What is there to say besides there isn't a chance in hell I can win this."

"How would you know without dealing the cards?"

I swallowed to relieve my dry throat. "Because you rigged this game the moment you learned about me."

"Is that when it happened?"

Hell, he'd all but admitted it. He wasn't a liar. I could give him that.

"Why do you want me, when you have women falling all over themselves for you?"

He moved closer to me, making my breath grow shallow.

"Because of the thought of sliding my cock into your mouth...your cunt...and your ass has haunted me from the moment I saw you on your knees in that botanical garden."

Visions of everything he said bloomed in my mind, and I couldn't help but lick my lips.

The closer he came, the faster my pulse hammered into my chest. A lightheadedness filled my head, and this need to run, to escape pushed at every nerve in my body.

Instead, I asked, "You want to marry another woman, so how can you expect me to agree to this?"

His hands gripped my waist, walking me backward until he had me pressed against the wall. "Who says you have a choice?

You want out of this marriage with a pristine reputation for yourself and your family, then I get you whenever, wherever, however I want for one year."

Tilting my head up, I tried to focus on his face and not the insanity of the arousal and panic coursing inside my body. "And then?"

"You get to live your life. Enjoy your secret club, your freedom." His piercing green eyes burned into mine. "We will fuck each other out of our systems, and I will return to New York and marry the woman I've chosen to fit into my life."

I clenched my jaw. "You're an asshole."

"This is a fact I never denied. It's probably the tamest of the things people call me."

"I'm not a whore." I pushed at his chest, and just as fast, he grabbed my arms, pinning them above my head.

"You will be my whore." His green gaze heated, and his lips tugged up at the corner before he added, "Until the end of our engagement."

The fact I wasn't offended by the idea, making me a complete dumbass, wasn't lost on me.

Desire pooled between my folds as the throbbing in my core grew to an almost unbearable ache, and the longing to press my thighs together intensified to the point where I had to force myself to stay still.

"This is extortion."

"Technically, it's blackmail."

"Blackmail," I echoed.

"Yes, that's the lie you can tell yourself every time I fuck you senseless." He leaned forward, bringing his mouth a hairsbreadth from mine. "And not because your body is dying for my touch, or because you're so desperate for me to make you come over and over again that you're going insane, or because you can't imagine going into your future vanilla life of freedom without a man like me dominating every inch of you. Inside. And. Out."

I couldn't breathe. Oh God, I couldn't breathe.

How the fuck could he know all of these things about me?

What was happening to me?

"You assume too much about me."

"Is that what you believe or what you want to believe?" He grazed his stubble-covered jaw along the sensitive curve of my neck, forcing my nipples to pebble into hard, unbearably aching peaks.

"You know nothing about me."

"Are you sure about that? All it will take is the slide of my fingers between the slick folds of your pussy lips to make a liar out of you."

As if hearing his words, my core contracted, and desire flooded my underwear.

"Tell me I have no effect on you. Tell me I'm just like any other man." He pressed his hard body to mine, his thick, steely cock a hot brand between us.

"It doesn't change anything," I whispered through an unsteady breath. "I don't want you, and you don't want me."

Well, maybe my body did, but hell if I'd voice that.

"What is so wrong with fucking each other to quench the need and then going our separate ways?"

"I won't let you trap me into a marriage. If anyone finds out we slept together, you have everything to gain."

"Haven't you figured it out yet, Goddess?"

"Figured what out?"

"You don't have a choice but to go through with this." He glided his mouth back and forth across mine.

It took all my effort not to moan.

"For your freedom, for your family's portion of the trust. You belong to me for the next year." He bit my lower lip, giving it a wickedly delicious sting that I felt deep down to the center of my being. "And to the matter of trapping you. If you kept your clubs a secret, I'm sure we can manage an affair without anyone being the wiser."

Fuck. I had to get away from him. He was too damn potent for me to think clearly.

I jerked my arms, trying to pull away, but his hold tightened and he lifted his head, that penetrating focus of his trained on me, telling me he saw way too much.

"You can always say no and chance the consequences. I'll lose the port, but think of all that you and your family will risk. Are you willing to put all of it on the line?"

"I hate you."

"I told you it wouldn't be the last time you'd say it to me."

I glared at him.

"But you want to know something else?"

"What?" I gritted out.

"I bet you're even angrier at yourself for how aroused you are at the thought of me fucking you, taking that cherry of yours, as Akari put it, of making you come every which way possible."

Refusing to admit he'd spoken even a word of the truth, I responded with, "The only reason I'm pissed off is because I'm in this situation. I reacted to you just like I would to any other good-looking man."

The lie lay heavy between us.

A glint of challenge lit his irises, and my heartbeat accelerated. This man read me without even trying. He understood my desires.

How was it possible to feel trapped and at the same time, desperate to stay trapped?

Shifting my wrists to one hand, he slid the large palm of the other down to engulf my neck, squeezing. The slight pressure sent a shockwave through my nipples, clit, and pussy.

Oh, dear God. I needed more of that.

I gasped, and then a guttural moan escaped my lips, betraying everything I'd spoken only moments earlier.

"Tell me, Goddess." His fingers tightened on my skin. "How many others caught your attention with a glance or made you want to squeeze your thighs together with the slightest pressure of his fingers to your wrists?"

I closed my eyes, feeling my walls crumbling under my traitorous body's desires. "You think too highly of yourself."

"It's called confidence. I know what I bring to the table. This is what you'll get from me. Raw, dirty, untamed. And one guarantee."

"And that is?"

He licked over my lower lip. "I won't be like any other lover you'll ever have again in your life."

It took all of my effort to hold in the whimper that sat on the cusp of my tongue.

This whole situation was so wrong on an infinite number of

levels, but the thrall this man weaved around me had sucked all common sense from my mind.

"One year only. You keep quiet about everything, and then you set me free."

"Is that an agreement to my proposal?" He set his forehead to mine. "Look me in the eyes and tell me, yes or no."

Lifting my lashes, I stared into emerald-like green irises.

This attraction, this lust, this desperate need pulsed out of every nerve in my body. In any other circumstance, I'd have jumped at the chance he offered.

"What's your answer?"

"You already know it. Was there really a choice, as you stated earlier?"

"There is always a choice."

"Simon." I couldn't hide the desperation in my voice.

"Say it." His fingers slid down my neck, between my breasts, making my nipples pebble to hardened points, and on to my hip.

My heartbeat hammered in my ears as I licked my lips and spoke the one word that would seal my fate for the next year, "Yes."

He remained still, holding my gaze as if assuring himself that he'd heard my answer correctly.

Just when I thought we'd stand there all night, he moved.

His lips crashed over mine, making me gasp and consuming my thoughts.

Holy fuck, this man was like a hurricane, setting each of my senses on fire and flooding my pussy with desire like nothing I'd encountered before.

He tasted incredible, cognac with a hint of orange peel from his drink, mixed with his own natural essence. No matter how much I tried to ignore it, the memory of him from last week had haunted me, making me wish for another sip. The kiss plunged me into an onslaught of sensation. The press of his hard, aroused body against mine was a heady mix I had no doubt I'd grow to crave.

His tongue rolled and teased, seducing, coaxing, and driving my need to an unbearable level just as he'd done with his words. This man was too overwhelming, too intoxicating, too much to take in at once.

I had to get some control. It was the only way to survive the next year.

I wasn't sure what came over me, but I broke the kiss, ignoring the fact I gasped for air, and ordered, "Release my hands. I'm as much part of this as you are."

"Is that right?" A cocky grin appeared on his face before he freed my arms and slid his palms down my body. "I think we need to establish something."

"What's that?" I challenged, setting my hands on his shoulders.

He gripped my thighs and lifted me against the wall while wrapping my legs around his waist. "When it comes to this agreement, especially when it comes to sex, you'll never be the one in charge. You better get used to it."

"We'll see, won't we?"

"Yes, we will." He captured my lips again, taking any response I could conjure with it.

Fuck.

Had anyone kissed me like this before? Dominating and giving at the same time.

His mouth trailed down my neck, leaving goosebumps in its wake. My nipples strained, and small spasms shook my pussy. I clutched at his shoulders, my heels dug into his ass, and I ground my aching clit along the hard ridge of the thick bulge of his fabric-covered cock.

A low groan vibrated from his throat, spurring a desperate ache unlike anything I'd experienced before.

What was happening to me?

He seemed to have a direct connection to my libido.

I hadn't even realized we'd moved into the primary bedroom until I found myself straddling Simon's thighs as he sat on the bed, and my sensitized front grazed against his hard chest.

The feral light in his emerald eyes mixed with the flush on his face, and the hard presence of his length against the damp crotch of my thong gave me the sensation of prey caught in the gaze of a predator. I wasn't sure whether to run or pull him closer.

He kneaded the muscles of my hips and thighs. "You're mine now."

"What does that mean?"

He answered by sliding his palms up the sides of my body and cupping my breasts in a possessive hold before pinching my nipples through the fabric of my dress.

"Oh God," I moaned and arched up into the pleasure-pain of his touch.

"It means…" He increased the pressure on my straining buds, heightening the euphoria sliding into my mind. "…this body is mine for the next year to do every dirty, depraved thing I want."

His fingers trailed to the front zipper of my dress, lowering it down until it stopped at the hem, splitting the garment open and leaving my underwear exposed.

"For a woman who's never had a lover, this is some sexy-as-fuck lingerie."

The way his eyes darkened, heating to an almost molten level, and then drank me in sent a shiver down my spine.

"I like pretty things. I wear it for me."

His voice was thick with arousal when he declared, "Now it's for me as well."

He pushed my dress from my shoulders and then drew me to him and trailed his mouth along my neck, over my collarbone, and down the valley of my breasts.

Oh, dear God.

My skin burned everywhere he touched, and I wanted more.

I closed my eyes and clutched at his muscled shoulders, needing to hold on to something. "Simon, what are you doing to me?"

"Seducing you," he murmured, unclasping my bra and pulling it free.

He returned to teasing and worrying my nipples, giving me a heady mix of almost too much and not enough sensation.

"What have you been doing for the last week?" I gasped out.

He gave me a wicked grin. "Setting a trap."

"Well, you caught me. There's no seduction necessary."

Fisting my hair, he tilted my head back. "That's where you're wrong. Seduction is always a factor. It doesn't matter if it is a fast, dirty fuck to relieve stress or slow, lazy morning sex. If it's not there, the man's not worth a grain of your time."

"So, you're going to train me for the type of lover I should look for in the future?"

"Something like that." A flash of irritation passed in his eyes as he spoke those words. "But for now, the only lover you need to think about is me."

It was so surreal to have such a casual conversation and to know we had a finite point to this relationship, or whatever it was.

And how within the last five minutes, I'd accepted this craziness.

All coherent thoughts evaporated the second Simon set his large hands on my hips and jerked me flush against his thick, hard cock and then ground it up and down my aching clit.

"Are you with me, Goddess?"

"Y…yes," I whimpered, clutching at his arms and closing my eyes, so lost in the sensations coursing through all my nerves.

"Take off my shirt."

The simple command had my heartbeat accelerating tenfold. "Okay."

I slipped from his lap and offered him my hand.

He studied my palm curiously before sliding his over it and standing.

With shaky fingers, I pulled his shirt from the waistband of his pants and slowly unbuttoned it, not understanding why I felt so nervous. As every inch of golden skin came into view, my breaths grew unsteady and the pulse of need throbbing deep inside my core climbed higher and higher. Arousal soaked through my underwear, giving me the urge to squeeze my thighs together.

I had no doubt he was well aware of how I reacted to him.

This man's body was exactly as I'd imagined.

Perfection. No, that wasn't the right word. Incredible.

He had honed and sculpted arms and muscled abs that I wanted to run my fingers over. Tattoos covered his skin along with scars, some small, others much larger. This wasn't the body of someone who worked with a personal trainer but that of a man who stood side-by-side with his men.

Toeing off his shoes, he set my palms on his belt. "Now the rest."

I swallowed, trying to push down the uncertainty bubbling up inside me.

I wasn't completely inexperienced, but no one I'd ever fooled around with held a candle to Simon. Hell, if they had, I probably wouldn't be a virgin now.

He confused me. Made me want him, even when I should hate him.

His hungry gaze ate me up as I meticulously removed his belt and then pants. The hard, heavy presence of his cock every step of the way posed a warning of how the night would end.

It was as if he knew prolonging the inevitable would heighten my arousal. He fucked my mind before he fucked me.

"Keep going," he coaxed, when all that was left was his underwear.

Inhaling an unsteady breath, I pushed the material from his hips.

"Now what?" I asked, but moved forward, taking him into my hand, stroking him from base to tip.

He felt hard, smooth, hot. All at the same time.

He threw his head back, a guttural moan escaping from his lips as his arm snaked around my waist.

"You're playing with fire, Goddess. And you are no way near ready for that."

I pumped him up and down, loving the feel of his steely length.

He pushed my hands away, picked me up, flipped me onto the bed, and then crawled over me.

"Do you always have to control everything?"

He nipped my jaw, sending a shiver down the column of my spine. "Yes. It's all I know."

"It's going to change with me," I murmured and tilted my neck to let him rub his stubble along my sensitive skin.

"Not a chance."

He moved lower, between my breasts, teasing and laving the nipples, then continued farther, biting the muscles of my stomach. I whimpered and gasped and then cried out as he scored his teeth along the inside of my thigh.

My core contracted in response to the pressure, and I fucking knew I was falling down a rabbit hole I'd never experience with any other man again. I wanted him to bite me. I wasn't sure how. I just knew.

Before I could ask him to make my thoughts a reality, he tugged my thong from my hips and pushed my thighs apart, exposing me completely to his view.

"I've wanted a taste of you all night. Now I get my chance."

The first swipes of his tongue had gasps escaping my lips, and with the next few, I was lost in the delicious newfound pleasure. Simon flicked, circled, teased my clit until I thought I'd go mad, and then he plunged one finger into my sopping pussy, curling upward.

As if my body waited for that extra stimulation, I detonated.

Everything inside me clenched and spasmed. My mind clouded as euphoria cascaded throughout every cell in my body.

Simon pushed another digit inside me and thrust in and out, forcing me to ride his hand as he continued to work my pussy with his mouth. He drove my orgasm higher, higher than I imagined possible.

"Simon, I can't. This is too much."

Ignoring me, he maintained his pleasure-filled torture, barely letting me come down before bringing me up for another wave of ecstasy.

Sweat covered every inch of me, and I could only gasp in the shallowest of breaths. I pulled at his hair, delirious, wanting him to stop and threatening to kill him if he dared to stop.

When he crawled over me, gloriously naked, condom on that seriously huge cock and hunger like nothing I'd seen in anyone's eyes, all I could think was that I had no regrets.

This may not have started out the way I wanted, but he wasn't a complete asshole. Not when it came to sex, anyway.

"We'll go slow," he said as the head of his cock sat poised against the entrance of my aching, wet pussy.

I couldn't help but smile up at him. "You do know I've masturbated before."

He narrowed his gaze.

"As in." I gripped the back of his head and pulled him to me. "With toys."

"Is that right?" He shifted forward, making me whimper as a tremor shot through my core.

"Yes."

"Then are you saying you don't want me to work my way

into you?" He slid in a portion of the way and then out, teasing me.

I dug my heels into his thighs, trying to urge him forward. "Yes, dammit."

"Then I guess there is only one thing to say."

I stared up into his emerald irises. "What is that?"

"You belong to me now, Goddess."

He slammed to the hilt.

"Oh, fuck," I cried out, back bowing.

This was nothing like having a dildo, at all. The sensation, the fullness, the warmth, the throbbing.

"Are you okay?" Simon gripped my jaw, forcing me to look at him.

"God, yes."

My response must have amused him because he shook his head. "Better than your toys?"

"The verdict is still out."

"Then let's make it so the jury comes back in my favor."

He sealed his lips over mine and set a rhythm meant to drive me insane. Just at the moment when I thought I would beg him to let me come, he rolled his hips in this perfect way, and I exploded around his cock, quivering and clenching.

"That's it. Show me how much you like it," he crooned into my ear. "Fuck. You're squeezing me so tight. Shit. I can't hold out any longer."

His fingers threaded in my hair in an almost brutal grip as his other hand grabbed a hold of my thigh, pulling it firm against his waist. His pace changed, growing harder and faster, almost as if something snapped inside him.

And for some reason, this loss of control and the intensity of his eyes as he stared down at me had my waning orgasm climbing again.

When I felt the sharp graze of his teeth on my neck, I cried out, "Simon, yes, please. God, I need more."

I arched and scored my nails across his shoulders, desperate for this insanity of what he was doing to my body.

He slid his fingers between our bodies to my clitoral nub, squeezing it between his knuckles. The pleasure-filled pain shot me into another wave of ecstasy and forced Simon into his own release.

The last thing I remembered hearing before I lost consciousness was, "What have I gotten into? You aren't supposed to like things the way I do."

11

SIMON

"ANY WORD ON THE SHIPMENT?" I ASKED KASEN AS I TOOK THE final steps from my plane onto the tarmac for private jets at JFK.

I buttoned my coat in an attempt to ward off the blistering late-January weather, walking in the direction of my waiting car.

"It's exactly where you expected our uncle and idiot cousin to hide it. I can't believe they thought we wouldn't look into the missing cargo."

"Leave it there. Let them think I don't know. Mykos is using his men to keep an eye on them by offering to assist in 'protection.'" I air-quoted.

"Mykos senior seems to want Albert's head on a silver platter."

"From what I've learned, it has to do with some personal insult from years past. Whatever the details, I'm not questioning it. We have a mutual interest in making sure Albert and Hal never gain any power. Ever."

"Speaking of mutual interests. You may want to spend more time in New York."

"Meaning?"

"People are starting to notice your extended absences over the last few months. You don't want to draw attention to your extracurricular activities, especially from her family."

"I have no plans to go anywhere this weekend. I am otherwise engaged."

Once seated inside my car, I sent a text to Nyx.

ME: *Landed. Remember the rules. I'll know if you cheated.*

NYX: *I don't follow rules. Haven't you figured this out yet?*

ME: *Then you'll have to deal with the consequences.*

NYX: *Been there, done that. If it wasn't for consequences, I wouldn't be in the situation I am in with you.*

ME: *You mean in a state of orgasmic haze whenever you're around me?*

NYX: *Apparently, you missed the memo this morning.*

ME: *I was running late.*

NYX: *Liar. Stayed long enough to get yours and then left me hanging.*

I smiled, remembering the death glare she'd given me when I'd brought her right on the cusp of coming with my mouth and then kissed her inner thigh, slipped from the bed, and walked out of her apartment to catch my flight.

"When does she get into town?" Kasen asked, drawing my

attention away from my phone and making me realize I had been completely ignoring him.

"This evening."

Tonight, every member of the Drakos and Mykos clans, as well as those we considered allies, would gather to make my engagement official. The dog-and-pony show would more than likely make me want to strangle my uncle for forcing the whole charade on me, but at least I'd end the night buried inside Nyx. Well, first, I'd have to make it past the armada surrounding the Mykos mansion in the Hamptons to Nyx's garden house.

"Told you she wasn't like anyone you knew."

Kasen's statement was a complete understatement. Nyx wasn't supposed to want and like the things I craved. Her sexual appetite went beyond anything I expected. Hell, she met me demand for demand. She took everything I gave her and then begged for more.

My cock jumped thinking of how she loved that edge of pain that seemed to border on too much. Never had a woman trusted me with her body to such an extreme level.

She brought out a side of me that made me want to fucking possess her. Which I had no doubt made me sound like a psychopath.

And then there was all the time we spent outside of fucking.

I actually enjoyed being around her. We talked, laughed, argued.

If anyone ever told me I'd look forward to going head-to-head with any woman, I'd have punched them in the face.

Maybe it was because Nyx couldn't give two shits about who or what I was. In fact, my status in my family turned her off. To her, it meant restrictions, rules, toeing the line. Everything she wanted to avoid with a ten-foot pole.

She definitely wasn't typical in any way.

Plus, the fact that until she moved to Vegas, she'd had as much decision power in her family business as her brothers and that she understood what it took to run Mykos Shipping, including the good, bad, and the dirty, made her no princess by any standards.

Then again, she wasn't a princess but a goddess.

I also figured out the only reason she allowed anyone to underestimate her was so they wouldn't look too closely at her other activities.

It was a clever-as-fuck guise, in my opinion.

What surprised me most was how freely she spoke about her gambling business with me. As if she felt comfortable letting her guard down since I knew more than most and I couldn't hold any more over her head.

I knew I was a bastard for blackmailing her into this, but I couldn't feel an ounce of guilt for it.

"She's definitely different." I glanced down at a braided black-and-red leather bracelet she'd bought from an elderly lady selling her handcrafted jewelry at a local craft fair on the outskirts of Vegas.

"You need to put some distance between the two of you." The order had me furrowing my brow and glaring at Kasen.

"How is this your business?"

Ignoring my question, he asked one of his own. "Have you realized outside of the week around the holidays, you've spent more time with her in the last few months than here in New York?"

I thought over his words, realizing he was right.

"Don't tell me you're still pissed about New Year's."

I'd let Kasen represent me at some ball in the Hamptons and decided to ring in the coming year in Vegas.

Lost in Nyx's body.

"She's not yours. Don't forget this."

I clenched my jaw, and said, "She is for one year. Officially starting tonight."

"You still need to keep some distance. Especially if this thing between the two of you is supposed to be a secret. Both of you are being reckless."

He had a point. And I could admit I hadn't made it easy to cover my tracks for the last few weeks. Normally, I'd have flown into different airports and then driven to my final destination.

However, this conversation revolved around more than making others suspicious of my involvement with Nyx. If anyone outside of the Mykos brothers found out about us, they wouldn't blink an eye, knowing we were engaged. But then again, letting anyone, specifically Albert and Hal, know Nyx had any significance in my life, outside of the business matters of this engagement, could cause more problems than I already dealt with.

Wait. Was I really thinking Nyx mattered more than business? Shit. Kasen needed to get out of my head.

"Lay it on the line, Kasen. What's the real reason that you want me to take a break from her?"

"Don't let her become your weakness. Don't get attached. Keep it casual. Business, as you planned from the beginning. It's better for the both of you when it ends."

The seriousness of his words had me pausing and going back to my thoughts from moments earlier.

What Kasen worried about wasn't possible. At least from my side. Nyx and I enjoyed each other, nothing more.

For me to have a weakness, I had to have a heart.

Gio Drakos had beaten it out of me long ago. To this day, his words remained etched in my head.

"Boy, I will make sure you won't destroy my legacy as your father did by marrying your mother. Now see where it got him. Dead. You will pick someone like your yia yia, *a woman who knows her place. Nothing is more important than the family."*

"You have nothing to worry about," I told Kasen. "Nyx and I want very different things for our lives. Besides, do you actually see the Mykos Hellion as my wife?"

"Without a question, and deep down, I think you're seeing it too."

"Well, you're wrong. The last thing I need is to worry about her private antics while trying to maintain control of the family and the territory. This is casual—no complications other than maintaining a low profile about our affair for the next year."

"Keep lying to yourself. The moment you flew to Las Vegas to see her three months ago, she became your undoing."

"Let me put this in terms you can understand. We fuck, we enjoy ourselves, and we go our separate ways. She believes this life of ours is a cage. Nyx wants her freedom, and I've agreed to give it to her. End of story."

Why did the thought of never seeing her after this year was up bother me so much?

"As I've mentioned before, I'll be here when it implodes."

12

Nyx

A LITTLE PAST EIGHT IN THE EVENING, I APPROACHED THE FOYER
overlooking the ballroom in my parents' Hamptons house, or
the more appropriate word for it was "mega-mansion."

It was all things grand, with large columns and opulence,
something one would see in the magazines to showcase the
super affluent and elite of New York.

The fact Papa hated the place always made me laugh. He
thought it was over-the-top pretentious and a waste of money.
From the moment he'd inherited it from my Pappous Steven,
he'd threatened to bulldoze the place to the ground and build a
bird sanctuary.

It really wasn't as bad as Papa believed. From the pictures I'd
seen, it was more on the gaudy, too-much-gold, and showy
side. Thankfully, Mama had convinced him to keep it and just

renovate the place, and now the family house, as I liked to call it, was grand but also welcoming and nothing like the monstrosity of before.

Okay, the main part of the house was comforting.

However, this room, I thought, moving closer to the ballroom, was another story.

From my spot, no one could see me, giving me the few extra minutes I needed to put my game face on.

The house was beautiful with its elegant chandelier and ivory drapes accenting the floor-to-ceiling windows. The snow drifting down in soft flutters around the shadows of the trees gave a soft and soothing vibe, meant to invite all the guests in for the celebration ahead.

However, we all knew this was a performance. The Drakos and Mykos history was turbulent at best and volatile at worst.

The current fakery taking place on the floor below sat on par with award-winning acting performances. If only I wasn't the one poised as the sacrificial offering for this Greek feast, I would have sat in my corner and laughed my ass off at the ridiculousness of it all.

"It's going to be okay, squirt," my brother Evan soothed as he approached and set a hand on my back. "Remember, this is all pretend."

"Pretend," I parroted. "And when it ends, I'm the one who'll have the ruined reputation. Don't they always blame the girl for a broken engagement?"

"Since when did you start caring about what anyone thought? Besides, can it get any worse than the Mykos Hellion?"

I cocked my head to the side, pursing my lips. "Keeping it real, as always."

"That's what I'm here for."

"So, what's the order of things tonight?"

"If you'd arrived yesterday as I suggested, you'd know."

He knew very well if it were any other family visit, I'd have arrived early and spent every waking moment with him or one of my other brothers. Evan and I were the closest in age, only two and a half years apart, and he was the one brother who understood me the best.

"What can I say, I'm a rebel. I don't follow instructions well."

Plus, with so many of our uncles, aunts, and cousins under one roof, the last thing I wanted to do was spend a single second more than I needed to with them and their demands I follow through with this wedding.

"Isn't that the truth." He studied me. "Something's different about you."

"Umm. Besides the fact I'm engaged to a guy I don't plan to marry?"

"Yes." He paused and then leaned close to my ear and whispered, "If you found someone, keep it under wraps. Don't let anyone find out about it. Not even Tyler, and especially not Drakos."

Of all my brothers, Evan picked up on things like crazy. Maybe it was because he was the enforcer for the family, and it was his job to watch out for things.

"Are you saying it wouldn't bother you?"

"Why the hell would it? This whole situation is bullshit. I don't even like Drakos, and it isn't fair to him, either. His uncle is a dick."

I tucked my arm into his and pressed myself to his side. "Did I tell you that you're my favorite brother?"

"Yeah, that will last all of five seconds and then you'll jump ship as soon as Tyler hands you a knife."

"I was a kid when that happened. You're never going to let me live that down."

"Never."

"Fine. I love all of my brothers equally, but you slightly more today."

"You are such a brat."

"Of course, I am. I'm the baby."

"Let's go." Evan tugged me toward the staircase leading into the ballroom.

As we made our way inside, I scanned the faces looking in my direction, many of them I knew and just as many I'd meet later.

"Don't even think about running."

"I'm not the type to run. I'm a Mykos."

"Damn straight. Don't ever forget it."

I held my chin up and let everyone take in their fill. I'd learned this game of rules and pedigree from the moment I took my first breath. I could play the debutante with the best of them.

I knew I looked damn good tonight. I'd gotten one of Akari's go-to designers to make a custom gown, and she hadn't disappointed. This dress hugged my body in all the right places, accentuating my long legs and curves without revealing too much.

And the dress had the added benefit of covering things I wasn't sure how to explain. I'd transitioned from never having had sex to weeks of almost nonstop fucking, eating, sleeping, and more fucking.

Well, maybe we engaged in some other things in between too, but the majority of our time was spent within the parameters of my penthouse. The only time my pussy got a break was when Simon made his infrequent trips to New York.

The man was seriously insatiable.

I released a deep breath, pushing down the pulse of arousal brewing to life inside me.

Dear God, Simon had turned me into a sex addict.

How the fuck was I supposed to pretend we were complete strangers when he'd seen me in every compromising situation possible?

I'd use my poker face, that's how. It helped me clean out the pockets of the biggest sharks in the world, so why not use it here?

As we moved into the crowd and continued to ignore most of our extended family, I said, "Just for the record, there is no one else. I don't have time for it."

Evan shook his head. "You've got to learn to live a little. What's the point of being in Vegas if you aren't going to have fun?"

"When was the last time you had fun, Ev?"

He led me in the direction where my parents waited. "That's something all of us siblings need to learn."

"I volunteer Tyler for the first sacrifice into the world of love and marriage, and then maybe I'll consider it."

"That will be a cold day in hell."

"You're probably..." I trailed off as my eyes connected with Simon's cool emerald ones from across the room.

Or maybe not cool, since I knew the heat the ice of his green irises hid. And the way he scanned me from head to toes increased the need pulsing in my body from moments earlier.

Okay, I had to get myself under control.

We were strangers. Not two people who'd fucked like rabbits the night before.

"I see the big bad wolf has caught your attention," Evan observed and then shifted as my family approached.

I had to force myself to look away. Damn man and his magnetic pull on my senses.

"Nyx, couldn't you have come even a few hours earlier? Your Papa was so worried you wouldn't show up," my mother admonished me in Greek before engulfing me in a tight hug. *"The least you could have done is come say hello before hiding away in your cottage."*

One of the perks of this insane property was my garden cottage, which was essentially a small house with two bedrooms, a living room, and a full kitchen. It was originally set up as the home for the onsite gardener, but Papa had gifted it to me with the attached greenhouse when I'd gone to NYU.

In fact, all of the siblings had separate houses on the property. This was a compound of sorts, though none of us actually lived here full-time.

"I'm sorry, Mama. You know it's better to keep a low profile after what happened at Christmas." I responded back in Greek, knowing she stayed calmer when we used our native language.

During the week I'd spent with my family over the holidays, we had our annual Mykos brunch, where my many aunts, including Aunt Teresa, decided to give me lessons on life. It was a complete disaster.

The few positives I could say about the event were that the food was incredible, and I wasn't the cause of drama.

Well, not technically.

"This is your engagement." Mama shook her head. *"There is no low profile. You are the center of it all. It is this idiot who needs to keep a low profile."*

She pointed to Tyler and glared. Okay, so speaking Greek wasn't going to work.

"She deserved it," Tyler chimed in as a crease formed between his brows.

I rolled my eyes. "I am very capable of defending my honor. You made the whole situation worse."

"The old bat suggested you seduce the asshole to lock in the marriage. What did you expect me to do?"

"Not engage with a crazy person." Evan added his two cents, which resulted in Tyler clenching his teeth.

Tyler would have completely lost his shit if he found out what had occurred the weekend before I'd come home for my visit or what would continue to happen for the next year.

Although everything ending in marriage would never, ever be in the cards.

I was no society wife, and Simon was too damn… ummm…*Simon.*

"Stop talking about nonsense and let me hug my baby girl before I have to hand her over to Drakos for the year."

"Umm, Papa." I hugged him and then whispered in his ear, "This is fake, remember?"

"Not as far as the world sees it. You have to make it look real."

"What aren't you telling me? Did something happen?"

He lifted his gaze to Tyler and Evan and then over to Nico, who'd arrived with Damon. "It is between Drakos and us."

A sadness washed over Papa's face that I couldn't understand.

"Since when am I not part of the discussion?"

"Since you decided that you wanted out of the discussion and our world," Tyler answered. "You can't have it both ways, Nyx. You're either in the business or not."

"You don't have to be a dick, Ty." Damon came over to me and took my hand. "This is why we wanted you to come early."

"No, I get it."

They'd always be my family, but the world I grew up in wouldn't be a part of my life once the year was out. I'd have to get used to it. No matter how much I hated the rules and annoyances, it was what I'd known.

"So, does this mean I have to act like the other princesses for the next year?" I asked Tyler with a smirk.

Relief washed over his face, and I realized he'd been worried about my reaction to the news. "The last thing any of us want is for you to be anything other than you."

"So, what now?"

"We meet your fiancé and your new in-laws."

I tucked my arm into Tyler's. "Lead the way."

"See, I knew you'd ditch me for him," Evan said.

I glanced over my shoulder. "You want to lead this crazy circus?"

"Not a chance. Ty can do the honors."

"Thanks, asshole."

"No, that's what they call her new fiancé."

God, I loved my family. No one outside of our circle of seven would believe my brothers and father were anything other than all-business, never-laughing, will-punch-you-in-the-face-rather-than-talk-to-you men. When in reality, they were fun-loving and complete morons half the time. Well, Papa wasn't, but my brothers, definitely.

As we made our way in Simon's direction, he separated from the group of people around him and moved toward me.

He watched me with almost a methodological fashion, as if I was something he had to figure out.

When I neared, the slight way he licked his lips caused my pulse to jump and my breath to grow shallow as I remembered what his wicked mouth had done to me on my kitchen counter this morning.

Fuck. This man had blackmailed me into sex, and now I'd become addicted. What a head trip.

When we stopped with only a foot between the two of us, his lips curved slightly when he said, "Hello, Olympia."

I narrowed my eyes, knowing he was fucking with me.

"My name is Nyx, asshole."

Tyler coughed, and I could almost hear my other brothers groan behind me, mixed with my parents' mortification.

Simon took my hand, drawing me closer to him, not caring this wasn't proper behavior.

Leaning in as if to kiss my cheek, he whispered, "I will pay you back for that, Goddess."

"You started it."

"There are still consequences."

"You'll have to make it past the guards on the property and around my cottage to do anything."

"Challenge accepted." He brushed his lips against my cheek, allowing the stubble of his beard to brush my jaw just a fraction and causing a shiver to slide down my spine.

He offered me his elbow.

After I slipped my arm into his and turned, he spoke in a tone only meant for my ears. "Time to make it official. Then, later tonight, you'll apologize for calling me an asshole in front of our families."

"It's good to keep hope alive." I glanced up at him with a smirk.

That was when I noticed my brothers all watching me as they followed behind us, curiosity and complete fascination etched on their faces.

My heartbeat accelerated.

I increased my pace, forcing Simon to keep up and put some distance between us and my family.

"Problem?" Simon asked with a little humor in his tone.

"I think we're acting too comfortable with each other. Maybe I should have been more of a bitch to you."

"Is that what you want to do? I'll play along, but remember I'll dish out as well as you can give."

"No. It's exhausting. Besides, it's not me. I do it to keep the vultures away."

"In a year's time, you won't have to worry about them ever again."

"If only that were true."

He tilted his head as he led me into the main hall area where the reception would take place. "Want to elaborate?"

"I may be out of the house, but the others like you will still circle."

"Meaning?"

"Simon, it isn't just my portion of the trust you get by actually marrying me. Didn't you do your research on me?"

"I assumed you had an inheritance from your father, but it wasn't something I was ever interested in."

"You really aren't like anyone I know. This is pretty much an open secret in the community."

"I don't listen to gossip."

"If I tell you this, don't you dare get any ideas. Is this clear?"

"I never go back on my word." I could tell I'd offended him, but I had to make sure he understood how I felt about this situation.

"Whoever I marry will have access to a portion of Mykos Shipping through me."

"Are you saying it's a dowry?"

"God, no. If you haven't figured it out by now, my family isn't the typical Greek family—dowries aren't in our vocabulary."

He stopped midstep, turning slightly. "You own a chunk of Mykos Shipping, don't you? You not only want to escape the society shit, but you also want away from the fuckers who think they can get a piece of your family's company by trapping you into marriage. That's why you keep saying I'll trap you."

"Men like you have end goals." I swallowed. "Money, power, standing. Everything is business. You stated it yourself—you are a replica of Gio Drakos, and his reputation was to expand his empire at any cost."

He narrowed his gaze. "We already established that you aren't the woman I plan to marry. And I have no need for your family's company."

"Then I guess we understand each other."

"I guess we do."

"We'll fuck, use each other, and then you'll set me free."

"Exactly."

———————

TWO HOURS LATER, I STEPPED OUT INTO THE SOLARIUM
overlooking the back lawn of the house. All the pretending and
nonstop chatter, including everyone's opinions about my
engagement, from family to random guests, had taken their toll.

I wasn't the younger version of myself anymore, the one
who'd mouth off and tell people where to stick their thoughts.
Moving to Vegas had taught me to put on what I called my
customer-service smile while envisioning lopping off their
heads with a knife or two.

Now, I was desperate for a stiff drink, but since it wasn't
becoming of a proper lady to engage in hard liquor in public, I
needed a few minutes alone, away from the watchful gazes of
my aunts, the society matrons, the socialites, and everyone else
who couldn't figure me out.

Not everyone here tonight disliked me or gave me a hard
time. Those friends couldn't understand why I'd agreed to this,
and I had no doubt they would try to corner me sooner or later.
Which gave me another reason to hide away in this room far
away from the hustle and bustle of the evening's events.

Though things had finally calmed.

Simon and I had gone through the formal engagement
charade from the introduction of family, dinner, then a final
ceremony where Simon had presented me with a ring.

We'd remained formal and remote after the conversation
about my inheritance, and in a sense, it had been for the best.
Wanting to stab him kept the lust at bay.

I glanced down at my engagement ring and shook my head. With its beauty and uniqueness, the piece had taken my breath away when he'd slid it on my finger.

It was exactly something I'd have chosen, unconventional and unlike anything one would see on every woman's hand. He'd given me a ring with a deep blue pear-shaped diamond surrounded by white diamonds.

The asshole pissed me off and then gave me something I would have wanted to wear if this was the real fucking thing.

I wanted to ask if he'd bought it or given the task to Kasen but kept those thoughts to myself, especially since I already knew the truth.

I wasn't supposed to like him. This wasn't supposed to be something fun, something I enjoyed, something I looked forward to when he was gone.

I released a deep breath as a lump formed in the pit of my stomach.

What the fuck had I gotten into?

I had to put some distance between us. I couldn't lose perspective. I couldn't let him fuck with my head. I knew better. My future involved a life away from all of this.

"Admiring your new jewelry?" a voice asked from the doorway to the solarium.

I lifted my head to find Camilla Santos with a group of women I assumed were her current entourage behind her. Her disdain for me showed in the few words she'd spoken, reminding me of her behavior all through high school.

This was one of the reasons I'd left. People seriously needed to grow the fuck up.

Maybe a small part of me could have mustered some sympathy for the fact she thought she'd lost her future husband.

Technically, I wasn't supposed to know Camilla was Simon's choice of bride. This tidbit of information wasn't public knowledge. However, to keep me from ever ending up in a situation where I was blindsided by unexpected information, my brothers had filled me in on all things Simon Drakos when our engagement occurred. This included his love life and future prospects.

I glanced at my ring again. "As a matter of fact, I was."

"I wouldn't get too comfortable. Let me fill you in on how things work with the Drakos men."

Okay, maybe I wasn't going to have any sympathy for her, after all.

13

SIMON

A LITTLE BEFORE ONE IN THE MORNING, I MADE MY WAY DOWN the hall to Nyx's bedroom. The sound of running water told me she'd just gotten in, and if I was lucky, I could jump into the shower with her.

I expected getting past the security on the Mykos property to pose a challenge, but what I'd encountered was beyond anything one would find on a family compound.

Fucking place was locked down better than Fort Knox.

Thankfully, my guys were there to help me out and gave me the heads-up on when to move. Then, the B&E skills I'd learned from a few choice friends aided me in entering Nyx's house.

As I slipped inside her bedroom, I heard the shower turn off and her move around the bathroom. A few seconds later, she stepped into the bedroom wrapped in a towel and then came to an abrupt stop, a scowl on her beautiful face.

"Why are you in my cottage?"

This hostility was the last thing I expected when I'd come through the doors a few moments ago.

Surprise, yes. Anger, no.

What the hell could have happened from the time I'd left to handle some business with my family and now?

Maybe she was still pissed about our exchange from earlier in the evening.

Ignoring her, I moved to lean against one of the tall posts of her giant bed.

"Let me repeat. Why are you in my cottage?"

"Want to tell me why you're so pissed at me?"

She pulled the terrycloth wrap from her hair, threw it onto a nearby chair, and narrowed her gaze. "How many women are you fucking right now?"

"At this very moment, I'm not actively fucking anyone."

She clenched her jaw. "How many women have you slept with since we started fucking?"

The vultures were already circling and getting in her ear, and she'd been in town less than a few hours.

"Does it matter, since this isn't a real engagement?"

She stalked to me and shoved me back while trying to clutch her towel to her chest. "If you believe I'm letting you put your dick in me while you're fucking other women, you've got another think coming."

But before she could shove me again, I grabbed her, pinning her back to my front.

"Let's get this straight." I reached for the belt of a robe

draped across the end of her bed. "My dick is going to make a permanent imprint in your cunt over the next year."

"Keep dreaming, asshole." She elbowed me in the stomach.

"I don't need to dream. It's a fact."

Before she realized what I was about to do, I tugged her arms behind her back and wound the silk around her wrists, causing her towel to fall to the floor.

"What the hell." She glared at me over her shoulder as she struggled against my hold. "I really hate you right now."

Her breath grew shallow and her eyes dilated as I cupped her face and brought my mouth to hers. "I'm sure you'll keep saying that for a long time to come."

As mad as she was, I knew the flush of her skin wasn't just from the blaze of anger.

She wanted to fuck.

I'd seen it the moment our eyes connected in the ballroom.

Hell, I'd seen it the first time I'd set eyes on her in Vegas three months ago.

The hunger, the arousal, the need. She was even more appealing now.

Wet hair tumbling all around her, naked, toned body warm from her shower, hands bound behind her back, and angry as a viper ready to make a meal of me.

All I wanted to do was bend her over her bed and take her until she submitted to every one of my demands.

A low whimper escaped her lips before she realized what she'd done and pulled back. "Simon, I swear to God, if you don't untie me, I will kick your ass."

"First of all"—I held her stare and challenged—"I'd like to see you try."

She clenched her teeth, ready to retort, but I spoke again. "Second, you're aroused by this, so don't even think about pretending you're not. I've fucked you enough to know you prefer the edge of pain over gentle any day. Actually, you want me to take it beyond the edge. Aren't you the one who likes to scream, 'bite me, choke me, just do something to make me come'?"

She swallowed but kept her lips pressed together.

The memories of her begging had my cock turning into a metal weight in my pants.

"And third, I'll untie you once I make something very clear."

I took her arms in one hand and gripped her hair with the other, tugging her head back. "You are mine to do with as I please. That's the deal. For my silence on your club activities, I get to fuck you, whenever, wherever, however I want."

"Like hell you do. Go ahead and try to prove I'm doing anything. As of now, Silent Night doesn't exist."

"Is that how you want to play it?"

"Yes," she whispered.

"That gentleman you held a knife to that first weekend we met will more than happily sing a nice tune to your activities. I can make sure of it."

"Keep dreaming. All I have to do is put the right words into the right ears, and he won't see another sunrise. You can't scare me with that shit."

"That's an even bigger risk you are taking. Is that the behavior of a morally chaste woman?"

"A morally chaste woman would never let you within a hundred feet of her."

"And we know I've been deep inside you. Every part of you.

Your mouth, you cunt, your ass." I bit the juncture at the back of her neck, where she already bore my mark. "Pounding into you. Making you beg. Making you come. Making you want more. I bet even now you're dripping for my fingers, mouth, cock."

Releasing my grip on her bound hands, I glided my palm over her waist, up her firm, toned stomach, and to her full naked breast.

A moan escaped her lips as I cupped and pinched her puckered nipple. "I hate you for making me want you when you're going to fuck other women."

"When did I ever give you any indication that I plan to fuck anyone besides you? And when the hell do you think I had the time to fuck someone else in the hours since I left your bed this morning and now?"

"You don't need to tell me. Your future bride and her entourage said plenty. Maybe I should take my cues from them and keep you as my side piece for the year and find the man I actually want when I'm in Vegas."

I tightened my hold in her hair, and a pained whimper spilled from her mouth. "The only man you'll fuck is me. Is that clear?"

Sliding my hand from her breast down to between her legs, I cupped her slick sex and gritted out, "I own this cunt. If you even think about letting anyone touch what is mine, I will eliminate them. Your father is known as the surgeon, but I'm darkness. There's nothing left to find when I'm done."

She shifted her bound wrists, grabbed my straining, fabric-covered cock, and held my gaze. "Then you better remember, if you put your cock in anyone else's cunt, I will not only kill them but you as well."

The intensity of her onyx stare and the fact there was no doubt she'd follow through with her threat, or at least give it her best shot, turned me on more than any other woman I'd ever encountered.

I never knew what I'd get from one moment to the next with her.

At times she was calm and sweet and then others, she was all brimstone and hellfire.

"Then I guess we have an understanding." I turned us until I positioned her toward the bed and pushed her forward, forcing her to drop stomach-down onto the soft duvet-covered mattress.

She glowered at me as I climbed over her and trapped her legs between mine.

"You're such an asshole."

"I never denied it." I toed off my shoes, shrugged out of my tuxedo jacket, threw it on the floor, and leaned down until my mouth grazed her ear. "But never forget this. You're the one who claimed exclusive rights to this asshole's cock for the next year. Now you have to live with the issues that come with the man attached to it."

"Stop talking and make use of the cock I claimed. If you'd fucked me like you should have this morning, maybe I'd be in a better mood and could have handled that bitch better."

"I'm positive you handled her adequately. Just like you do everything. Besides"—I grazed the stubble of my beard along the column of her throat, causing goosebumps to prickle her neck and making her breath quicken—"you haven't earned my cock."

"The hell I haven't." She arched her neck as her eyes grew

heavy-lidded. "I showed up to an engagement party I never wanted, dealt with both sides of our families, handled your lady love and her crew detailing your extracurricular activities, and have managed the whole day with a case of lady blue balls. You should be showering me in diamonds for not slitting anyone's throat tonight."

"You want diamonds, Goddess?" Shifting back, I untied her wrists, pulled her left hand up, and set it above her head within eyesight. "Isn't this big enough?"

She was quiet for a second. "It's beautiful. I'm surprised it's something I'd actually want to wear. Who picked it? You or Kasen?"

Why the hell would she think Kasen would choose something for her?

"It was my mother's."

Fuck. What possessed me to confess something like that to her?

"Why would you give me a ring that has sentimental value to you?"

I'd wondered the same damn thing.

Who was I kidding?

I couldn't see Nyx wearing anything traditional or what every other socialite would have worn on her finger.

Then I'd remembered Mama's ring and known it was perfect for Nyx.

Mama had caused a stir when she, a lowly, opinionated librarian, had married Papa. From my memories of her, she'd taken no one's shit, even when keeping quiet would have made life so much easier for her.

It made sense to give the ring of a rebel to another rebel.

It was crafted with a combination of a rare fancy intense blue diamond and flawless white diamonds, worth a small fortune. From what I remembered my father telling me, he'd won it in a game of poker.

Definitely a fitting ring for Nyx.

"As far as the world at large knows, this is the real thing," I informed her. "Giving you Mama's ring makes it believable."

She grew quiet again, curling her fist and thumbing the white and blue diamonds before she said, "That sounds reasonable."

"Now we need to return to the previous conversation."

Twisting her body to face me, she grinned at me. "You mean about showering me with diamonds?"

"No, about making you earn my cock."

The flush on her face deepened, and a crease formed between her brows, telling me she was up to something. "We need to get something straight."

"Is that right?"

"Yes. I don't need to earn anything. You came here for a purpose. Either get to it or get lost. I took care of myself before you. I can do it again."

I grabbed hold of her hair, jerking her head back, and a low whimper of desire escaped her lips. "Well, before I get to it, as you put it, let me remind you of something you haven't quite grasped yet."

Pushing my knees between hers, I slid an arm around her waist, forcing her up while maintaining my hold in her wet tresses.

"I'm never going to be the man you can control, Nyx Mykos." I scraped my teeth along the column of her neck and then bit down on the same point where she bore the marks of a fading bruise from a session when she'd begged me to make it hurt as she orgasmed.

"Oh God, Simon." She cupped the back of my neck as her other hand kneaded the muscles of my thigh through the fabric of my pants.

"You need to remember, if I give in to you, it's because I want to and it's for a purpose." I brought my palm from her stomach, through the lips of her soaked sex, and rimmed her pussy, giving her no more than the barest tease of two fingers. "The power you have is what I give you."

"You...you want to take everything from me and give nothing back." She dropped her head, closing her eyes.

She had no idea everything I'd just said was bullshit. She had all the power. Soon, she'd figure it out.

"I'm going to give you your freedom."

"Please don't break that promise."

The way her lips trembled as she'd spoken those words made me realize how much she viewed marriage as a trap.

Fuck.

I was the one who should be worried about this shit, not the opposite way around.

I plunged knuckles-deep into her slick pussy, thrusting in and out. Her back bowed, and a guttural moan escaped her lips as her long nails scored the skin on the back of my neck.

"You have nothing to fear. Even if you fall in love with me, I won't break my promise."

Why the fuck did those words sound like a lie to my ears?

I was seriously losing it today.

Her palm settled over the hand I had between her legs, pausing my movement. "What if you're the one who falls?"

Pulling free of her body, I gripped her hips and flipped her onto her back. God, she was beautiful, cheeks flushed, breath shallow, and eyes dilated with the haze of lust and arousal.

"My falling in love is something you'll never have to worry about. In fact, there isn't a chance in hell of that happening."

She lifted her chin. "Why is that?"

"Because I don't have a heart. As I told you, I'm Gio Drakos's creation. Having a heart means I have weaknesses."

"And you can't have any," she added. Something like sadness passed in her eyes but disappeared just as fast.

I nodded.

"Then I have nothing to fear." She fisted my shirt, drawing me to her. "This is just sex."

14

SIMON

I STARED INTO NYX'S LUST-GLAZED EYES, NOT UNDERSTANDING what was happening to me.

Her easy acceptance of our situation, of my never being able to love her, of us having an end date, of this being just sex, left uneasiness in the pit of my stomach.

What the fuck was wrong with me?

"This is more than just sex, Goddess."

A crease formed between her brow. "What label would you put on it, then?"

I kissed her, biting her lower lip and giving it a hard enough pinch that it would leave it swollen. "It's hot, dirty, depraved sex that leaves you bruised at times and requires you to wear dresses designed specifically to hide the marks left over from our activities."

Her frown disappeared as her lips tugged up, and she touched the spot where I'd bitten her a few minutes ago. "Not sure how I could have explained it to my parents or brothers."

"You asked for it."

"I did." She brushed her naked body against mine. "Do it again."

The way her voice grew heavy with lust had my cock ready to break free of my pants, and I tugged her flush to me.

Leaning over her and caging her with my arms, I stared down at her. "You make no sense, Olympia Nyx Mykos. Never have I met a woman like you. You're fascinating as fuck."

Her face broke out into a big smile, transforming her from the beauty she already was to the goddess I called her. "I think that's the best compliment anyone's given me."

"You'd rather be fascinating than beautiful?"

"Hell, yes. Beauty is fleeting. I'd rather be someone notorious and memorable."

I stared down at her, feeling the knot in my stomach tighten. For a split second, I could almost hear Kasen's warning in the back of my head. *"She's not yours."*

The hell she wasn't.

Pushing my thoughts back, I focused on the woman in my arms. "Then you definitely achieved your objective. There is no one else like you. Can we stop talking and fuck?"

She pursed her lips together, trying to hold in a smile, and then nodded, wrapping her arms around my neck.

There were no more words as we lost ourselves in the intoxication of each other's mouths, savoring, tasting, enjoying.

Her fingers pulled at my clothes, searching out skin and making me gasp as her nails scored up my abs.

"If I can handle bruises and bites, you can handle scratches."

"That's not how this works. Besides, you beg for those."

Grabbing hold of her hands, I took the belt of her robe, weaved it around her wrists, and then tied it to one of the posters of her bed.

As I stepped off the bed, she glared at me, desire and annoyance weaved together.

"Don't you dare leave me hanging again."

I began to shuck my clothing and held in a grin. "I had to work my way around an army of security to reach your front door. I'm not leaving without fucking you."

"Then get to it, Drakos."

Only she would give orders, even bound and stretched out like a sacrifice on a bed.

Never had a woman made me laugh during sex. There were a lot of nevers and firsts with her.

Kasen's voice echoed in my head again. *Don't let her become your weakness. Don't get attached. Keep it casual. Business, as you planned from the beginning. It's better for the both of you when it ends.*

"Simon? Why are you staring at me like that?"

My mind snapped back to the goddess in front of me, and I crawled over her, grasping both of her ankles and pulling her pussy flush against my straining cock.

"Oh God." A moan escaped her full lips, and she threw her head back.

Leaning forward, I braced an arm near her shoulder and collared her throat with my hand. "You're mine, Goddess."

She shifted her hips, rubbing her slick pussy against the head of my aching cock. "Fuck me and stop talking."

"Did you hear me?" I rimmed her without giving her the penetration she craved.

A mewled whimper escaped from her mouth before she begged, "Simon, please."

"You have to answer me first."

Her gaze connected with mine, something passing in the black depths, and she shook her head. "This is temporary."

I increased the pressure on her neck, watching her gaze dilate and breath grow shallower.

"For now, you're mine, body, mind, and soul."

"No, all you get is my body. This is business wrapped in blackmail, remember?"

Just as I was about to tell her how things worked in this relationship, she hooked her legs against the back of my hips and with one swift arch of her pelvis, impaled herself on my dick.

"Goddess," I called out, clenching my teeth.

This woman was going to kill me.

"I said, stop talking."

I dropped my forehead to hers, and my hold on her throat tightened as I pulled out to the tip of my cock. "You want to fuck?"

"Yes."

"Then that is exactly what we will do." I slammed into her, making her gasp. "When we're done, you'll feel me with every step."

"Please," she whimpered, and I closed my eyes, wondering why nothing I said turned her off.

Instead of focusing on it too much, I shifted, gripped her

hips, adjusted her to that perfect angle, and set a hard, relentless pace.

As if this was all she waited for, she clenched her eyes tight and screamed, "Yes, Simon. More. Give me more."

God, she was so beautiful. Face flushed, nipples puckered into tight buds, and body glistening with sweat. I could watch her forever.

"What do you want, Goddess?" I rolled my hips in that way she liked but only enough to tease her.

Her pussy quivered and flooded my cock as she thrashed her bound arms against the post above her head.

"Anything, do something to send me over. Stop torturing me." She ground her heels into the mattress and tossed her head side to side.

Reaching forward, I untied her hands. Immediately she wrapped her arms around my shoulders and arched up against me. I fisted her hair again, tilting her neck, and grazed my teeth along the spot she loved for me to clamp down on.

"Fuck, Simon, just do it."

At the same moment I bit down, I slid my fingers between her pussy lips and took hold of her swollen clit, giving her an extra edge of pain she loved.

Her body erupted. She gasped and moaned incoherent words, raking her nails down my arms and back. Her pussy flooded my cock with her arousal while clamping down so hard that I could barely move inside her.

I continued to pump into her, bringing her over the cusp two more times, and then I let my beast out, not caring if the guards patrolling outside heard us.

When I finally came, I knew two things.

First, I had to convince Nyx to take back the promise that I'd made her because I fucking planned to keep her.

And second, I hoped to God when everything came out, I didn't start another war that would take a century to end.

A LITTLE BEFORE DAWN, A MESSAGE SOUNDED ON MY PHONE alerting me it was shift change for the security around the Mykos estate. Which meant I had to leave Nyx's bed and make my way off the property.

I glanced down at Nyx's head pressed against my bare chest and her delicate, naked body curled along mine.

The thought of leaving her pissed me off. Maybe it was the fact I'd gotten used to spending so much time with her that this had become our routine.

No. Our routine had been me fucking her unconscious and then us going about our day. Her to the botanical gardens and me to the office in her penthouse to work.

I tucked a stray hair behind her ear and shook my head.

She was a hellion, but not the kind everyone wanted to depict. She wouldn't fit the mold, and it was obvious at the party that her refusal to conform made her a target.

And I couldn't understand why Camilla would tell Nyx I was going to fuck around on her. As far as the world at large knew, Nyx and I were set to marry, and Camilla had no chance. Pulling this shit had to have some ulterior motive.

My gut said her father, Kes Santos, was behind this. I'd assigned some of my men to investigate the fucker once I left here.

Nyx shifted, and her hand slid from my upper chest, down my abdomen, to just above my groin, making me close my eyes as my cock stirred to life.

This was not the time for it.

My phone beeped again, and I knew I had to move or risk one or all of the Mykoses showing up. From the information my team had relayed, all of the brothers had arrived on the property this morning for brunch with their parents.

Maybe Nyx was different because her family was. The Mykoses spent time together like normal families. Well, normal, non-syndicate families who weren't forced to be together because of an order or duty.

They enjoyed each other's company, spent time together outside of business and obligations. Maybe it was an exaggeration, but Nyx swore her father started to pout if she didn't visit him once a month or more. The last thing anyone would expect the Mykos Surgeon to do was pout.

Their family shared a type of intimacy and bond I couldn't understand.

No, that wasn't true. I'd had somewhat of a normal life up until my parents' murder. With Gio as a grandfather, no one could claim anything as typical. But my mother had done her best to keep simple things a part of our life, from dinners every evening to afterschool activities both parents attended.

My phone beeped with an incoming message.

KASEN: *Get your ass up. You need to pack a bag. We have shit to deal with that needs your undivided attention.*

A second later, a picture of a burning half-finished ship appeared on my phone.

Well, that was just fucking great.

ME: *Tell the pilot to ready the jet. I'm on my way. Was it Albert?*

KASEN: *My gut says either Albert or Hal. As of now, we need you to get your ass to Greece.*

ME: *On my way.*

Sighing, I set my phone to the side, unwrapped myself from Nyx's heat, and rose from the bed.

"When are you coming out to Vegas again?"

"I'm not sure. I'll let you know as soon as I deal with some business issues. It may be one to two weeks, possibly more."

"Issues." She sat up, tucking the sheet around her chest. "I see."

The coolness of her tone had me pausing.

"What do you see?"

"You want me to believe that you aren't going to fuck around."

"Yes."

She closed her eyes, turning her face away from me. "Don't lie to me, Simon. I'd rather you just lay it out for me. I know how men like you operate."

"Want to explain what 'men like you' means?"

"I grew up in this world. I've seen it all and heard it all."

I climbed on the bed, caging her with my body. "I thought we cleared this up last night. The only person I plan to fuck is you. And the only person you will fuck is me."

"You're going to go more than two weeks without sex?"

"No, I'm not."

She narrowed her gaze, but before she could say anything, I spoke. "The longest I'm planning to go without being in your tight cunt is two weeks, tops, if that."

"Are you saying that you're going to fly out between whatever issues you are handling to come fuck me?"

"That's exactly what I'm saying."

"It will get old. Especially with your busy schedule."

"Is that a challenge, Ms. Mykos?"

"It is, Mr. Drakos."

"Challenge accepted."

"And how are you going to explain your trips to the world?"

"I'm going to let them believe I'm having an affair. But it just so happens, the affair is with my fiancée."

15

NYX

"EXCUSE ME, MS. MYKOS. THERE IS A MR. DRAKOS ASKING FOR you."

I glanced up from my supply order paperwork to focus on one of the Ida botanical garden attendants, who stood in the doorway of my office.

"Thanks, Janice. Let him know I'll be out in a few moments."

She nodded and then left.

I frowned and checked my phone, knowing I couldn't have missed a message or call from Simon. Then again, over the last five weeks, our communication had shifted from long phone calls to none all day, and the sexy text banter I'd gotten so used to had turned into one-or-two-line messages with no discussion of visits or anything other than future formal events.

The trips he'd mentioned to come see me every two weeks had never occurred. The only explanation he'd given me involved some crap about negotiations that required nonstop attention or they would fall through.

What kind of negotiations took five weeks?

Hell, we hadn't even seen each other when I'd visited my family for my monthly New York trip.

Something had changed, and I couldn't understand what had shifted. He'd placed this boundary between us, making it very clear that he'd decided it was better to end the physical aspect of our relationship.

Asshole couldn't even tell me straight to my face that he was ending it.

Bastard.

Maybe it was a good thing.

The pull I felt for him had started to muddle my head, and I couldn't let myself become attached. I had a goal, and he would complicate things, forcing me to blur the lines.

Pulling out my phone, I sent Simon a text.

ME: *Hey, asshole. Since when did you learn manners and request permission to speak to me? Don't you just walk into the employee side of the gardens and demand my attention?*

Almost immediately the three dots started moving.

SIMON: *I have no idea what the fuck you are talking about. I've been in negotiations for the last five hours.*

ME: *Then which Mr. Drakos is here to see me?*

SIMON: *I have no fucking idea, but I'm about to find out. Don't you dare go see anyone.*

ME: *Haven't we already established that I don't follow directions well? Especially ones given by jerks who get sticks up their ass, cut off communication, and decide I'm not worth their time.*

SIMON: *If you step one foot away from the security of that garden, I swear I will make your ass so red, you'll regret it.*

The threat of him touching my ass had my body heating.

Get it together, Nyx. It's over.

ME: *That would require you to be in the same place I am. Which you aren't.*

SIMON: *Don't test me, Goddess.*

ME: *I'm not your goddess, I'm not your anything. And for the record, if I can handle one asshole Drakos, I'm capable of handling any other.*

SIMON: *Is that what you think you're doing? Handling me?*

ME: *Actually, I don't want to handle you, at all. I don't want anything to do with you.*

SIMON: *You're going to do a lot with me when I get to you. Especially if you don't listen to what I'm telling you.*

ME: *We're texting, not talking. I can't hear a damn thing you're saying, asshole.*

Almost immediately, my phone rang. The spiteful side of me wanted to let it go to voicemail, but the idiot part of me answered.

"What do you want?" I barked into my phone.

"You're going to do as I say, Goddess." The way he spoke those words reminded me of another time he'd used that exact phrase, commanding me to drop to my knees and suck him off.

My traitorous body reacted, and I bit the inside of my cheek instead of focusing on how my nipples pebbled and my pussy grew slick.

Through gritted teeth, I said, "Don't."

"Don't what?" He let his voice do that thing that intensified the ache deep in my core.

"You already made it clear you're done with me, so stop fucking with me."

"Is that what you think?"

"It's what I know. I'm a big girl who's familiar with how things work."

"That's surprising since I'm the first man who's ever touched you, who's ever fucked you, who's ever come inside you." I closed my eyes, hating the way I wanted this fucker. "What gives you the impression I'm even remotely finished with you?"

I shifted my phone to the other ear. "Your actions."

"I was handling business. Business that I wish to hell I could hand off to someone else without causing more chaos."

"I don't care."

"Liar. You're wondering who I put my dick in for the last five weeks. Want to know the answer?"

"I don't have time for your mind games." I pressed my fingers to the bridge of my nose. "Get lost. I have work to do and a different Drakos to get rid of."

"You will not see him. That's an order."

My temper was piqued. "Listen up, dickhead. I don't take orders from you. You aren't my father. You aren't one of my brothers. You are my fake fiancé who I used to fuck. Hear that. Used. To. Fuck. You have no say in my life. Now fuck off, Drakos. I have things to do."

I hung up, set the phone down, and closed my eyes for a moment, knowing I'd done the one thing I shouldn't have. I'd gotten attached.

Shit. Shit. Shit.

I had gotten attached to the dickhead, and it hurt like hell that he'd ghosted me.

It was better to deal with it now than to question everything later. I had to remember he represented everything I hated about the world I'd grown up in. The rules, the expectations, the pretenses.

I wanted a normal life, a normal job, something away from the craziness I'd grown up around, with someone who accepted me the way I was, someone who wouldn't want me to fit a mold, someone who wanted me for me, someone who put me first, or at least on the priority list.

Maybe seeing my parents had spoiled me. Papa and Mama had fallen in love as teens but were expected to marry different people. Then on the day of Mama's wedding, Papa stole her away. It had caused a huge scandal, but in the end, another scandal overshadowed theirs and people forgot about it.

Well, except the fact Mama was the greatest weakness of the man known as the Mykos Surgeon. Papa never shied away from saying that he would burn the world down if anything happened to Mama. That was probably why he made sure she had protection around her day and night. At times, I felt he went overboard, but Mama always seemed to find ways around it.

In fact, I'd learned a few of my tricks from her.

Thinking of tricks, I had to find out who out of the Drakos clan wanted to see me. Simon had made it pretty obvious he wasn't privy to the information.

I rose from my desk and made my way out of the back side of the gardens. Standing next to a collection of tall flowering hibiscus trees stood a man with Simon's similar height and build. The style of clothing looked almost the same, as well, except this guy seemed to have the edge of vanity where the designer labels were prominently displayed on his shoes and belt, whereas Simon wore clothes everyone knew were custom made and needed no labels.

As the man's face came into view, I recognized him as Simon's younger cousin, Hal. This made no sense. From what Tyler relayed about Simon's cousin, they hated each other on a good day. Simon hadn't even introduced me to him or his Uncle Albert at the engagement party.

Something about him seemed off, as if he knew he wasn't supposed to be anywhere in the vicinity. His gaze scanned the area constantly. That's when I noticed the poker chip he twirled between his fingers, and my heartbeat accelerated.

It was one of the ones I used for the Silent Night events. It had the custom moon-and-stars emblem engraved in it, representing the ancient goddess of night.

We accounted for every chip at the end of an event. Covering our asses was a priority. And the only time a chip had gone missing since I started running my events at the age of eighteen was after the night David had played against the Middle Eastern royals I told him not to even consider approaching.

Now, Hal Drakos had possession of it. Which meant he wanted something from me.

Fuck.

Pulling out my cell, I sent a message to Stevie and informed her that I'd located the missing chip. Immediately, she responded.

STEVIE: *Either tell your fiancé to handle it, or you need to come clean to your brothers. I'm sure they will take great pleasure in handling it their way.*

ME: *Getting them to fix my problems means I'm tied to their world.*

STEVIE: *When are you going to realize it's your world too? It's not something you can just decide to leave, no matter what you believe. Besides, what you do isn't exactly toeing the line. If you really wanted a normal life, you'd have to become an actual flower shop owner, or maybe a college professor.*

ME: *Can we keep the lectures to a minimum at the moment? There are other priorities we need to focus on. Maybe I should meet with him and find out what the fuck he wants.*

STEVIE: *That's a bad idea on an epic proportion.*

I sighed. Not a second later, another message came in.

STEVIE: *I'm sending Tony over. He'll keep watch over your fake future in-law. Get your ass back in here.*

Damn. Stevie was seriously bossy when in protector mode.

Less than thirty seconds later, Tony stood before me, completely blocking me from Hal or anyone's view. The concern on his face had me pausing a smartass remark I was about to make.

"Nyx, you need to follow orders and get back inside. With the shit going on in Drakos's house, the last thing we want to do is make you a target."

I wanted to probe him for more information, but I was positive he wouldn't give it to me. Especially if Tyler or Papa had told him not to say anything.

A lump settled in my gut.

This is how this would continue when I stepped away from

everything. I'd remain part of the family but separate. Never again a member of the inner circle. Never again the one to give Papa or my brothers a perspective outside of the day-to-day operations of the organization.

Releasing a sigh, I pushed the melancholy down. I turned back toward the garden offices and made my way inside with Tony close behind me.

"You can always change your mind." Tony's gentle words caused an ached to bloom in my chest.

"I don't know what I want anymore."

"Is it because of Drakos or your family?"

"Drakos has nothing to do with it. We're over." Just saying that left a sour taste in my mouth.

"I wouldn't be so sure about that."

I glared at him over my shoulder. "I am. Can you arrange for a jet to take me home? I want to see my family."

"So, you're finally going to tell them? It may be for the best."

"No."

"Then tell Drakos about the chip."

I shook my head. "Nothing on the chip can link directly back to me. All it has is the emblem of the club. Let him have it. If I don't put up with shit from the one I'm engaged to, I'm not going to do it from this one."

"Then in the meantime, I'm going to double your security. I'd rather err on the safe side of caution." The no-nonsense way Tony had spoken those words made me want to laugh.

I nodded, acquiescing. "Why do I get the feeling you're about to put me in a twenty-four-hour surveillance situation like you did when I snuck out of the house to scare Teresa for stealing my broach?"

Tony kept his stoic expression except for the slight twitch of his lips. "Because you're just as much trouble now as you were then."

16

NYX

TWENTY-FOUR HOURS AFTER LEAVING VEGAS, I WALKED OUT onto the heated patio leading to the greenhouse connected to my cottage. It was a little past one in the morning, and no matter how hard I'd tried, sleep seemed to elude me.

Stupid time zones.

Usually, a little digging in the dirt calmed my mind and helped me relax enough to get a few hours of shut-eye before the giant brunch my parents always planned whenever the five kids were in town at the same time.

Opening the glass doors, I stepped into the warm, balmy room and inhaled the air, taking in the rich, earthy essence of the place. There really was nothing like the smell of plants, flowers, nature. My brothers never understood my fascination with nature, but for as long as I could remember, I'd loved to watch things grow.

I made my way into the deepest part of the greenhouse, where I kept my supplies, and began to strip out of the outer layers of my clothes until all I had on was my robe and nightgown.

Stretching my arms wide, I spun around in a circle. God, I loved it in here.

If I wanted, I could flip cartwheels or run around butt naked in here, and no one would blink an eye. This was my safe space, my sanctuary. A place to think and regroup.

Which was what I needed to do now.

Earlier tonight, some of my old friends had gathered at a local club for a fun evening where we reminisced about our past and our college antics. We drank way too much and laughed too hard. It felt freeing, but the lump in my stomach hadn't eased.

Instead of worrying about Hal having the poker chip David stole from one of my games, my emotions were all twisted over a man who was doing heaven knew what, at the moment.

Fucking Simon.

This whole situation was so wrong, and even knowing nothing would have come of anything between us, I couldn't help but feel salty about how he'd treated me.

Asshole.

Yes, that's what he was. A fucking asshole for not being straight with me.

Next time I saw Akari, I planned to tell her to take her advice and shove it up her butt.

I jumped at the sound of the greenhouse door creaking

behind me, and before I realized I'd moved, I grabbed a blade from the butcher block table near me and threw it at the door, embedding the steel into the doorframe.

"Fuck, Goddess. Is that how you greet every guest?"

My heartbeat echoed into my ears as I stared at Simon's face. "Unwelcome ones. I didn't have to miss."

Anger radiated into every nerve in my system. How dare he walk into my greenhouse after his five-week stunt.

And why the hell did he have to look so fucking good?

"I'm sure you didn't." Simon stepped inside, shutting the door and then locking it behind him. "But I'm happy you did."

"I don't want you here." I shifted, moving slightly backward.

"Does it look like I care?"

"You should care. It could end badly."

"Why is that? Are you planning to throw more knives at me?" His eyes heated, sending a shiver down my spine and making me want to smack myself for always having some type of physical response to him.

I took another retreating step as my breath grew shallow. "If my family finds you here with me, they'll kill you."

"That's the last thing that would happen if they found us together, and you know it." His lips tugged up at the corner. "Who was the Drakos that came to see you?"

It was on the tip of my tongue to tell him, but then I decided to keep it to myself. The chip was inconsequential, and I wouldn't let myself become a pawn in this thing between Simon and his cousin.

"I never met with him."

"You actually listened?"

"Sometimes, I can be accommodating."

He nodded, and I wasn't sure if he believed a word I was saying. "I went to Vegas. You weren't there."

"Wh...why would you go there?" I couldn't hide the confusion in my voice.

This made no sense. He'd dumped me.

He stalked forward, his green eyes growing molten like a predator ready to devour his prey.

"My original plan was to make a pitstop here to freshen up before I caught another flight to see you, but our phone call altered things."

I lifted my hand in a futile attempt to ward him off and continued to move backward. "You made it clear we're over, remember?"

"Did I? Or did you make an assumption?"

I lifted my chin. "It was deductive reasoning."

"Well, let's reason something else out."

He moved so fast, coming upon me and pinning me to the iron lattice on the wall, that I could barely squeak out a gasp.

I grabbed hold of his forearms, unable to do anything else as the intensity of his presence overwhelmed my senses.

"Do you know what I wanted to do after spending nearly every waking hour for over a month in Thessaloniki dealing with one bullshit situation after another?"

His negotiations were in Greece? This meant he was dealing with the ports and all the builders. Why would he keep this from me?

Instead of asking him my questions, I responded to his question. "What?"

"I wanted to lose myself in your body. I wanted to talk to

you about stupid shit and fucking argue with you just so you'd threaten to slit my throat."

His words had a tinge of panic bubbling up.

"This isn't a real relationship, Simon. We used to fuck, nothing else."

"You are mine, Goddess. I made that clear that first night together over four months ago. And when it comes to fucking, there is no 'used to' about it. The agreement is one year from the engagement." His hand slid up to my neck as the other crept around my waist, making my breath accelerate and desire flood my core. "Those ninety or so days prior aren't part of the equation. That means I have eleven more months to do with you as I please."

"If that's true, then you need to figure out this hot-cold shit. I won't put up with it."

"Is that right?" He tilted my head to the side, grazing his teeth along the column of my neck, and then bit down, giving me the pleasure-filled pain I craved so much.

I cried out and then whispered, "I hate you for using my body against me when I mean nothing to you."

"Are you saying I matter to you?" He lifted my hands from his arms and wrapped my fingers around the metal bars above my head.

"I won't let you matter. This is physical, nothing more."

"Physical," he parroted, as his palm glided down my throat to cup my breast before he pinched my puckered nipple between his thumb and index finger.

"Oh God, Simon."

He moved closer to me, his thick, hard cock a heated brand between us.

"Tell me, Goddess," he said, increasing the pressure. "Did you ache for me, for my touch, for my mouth, my cock?"

I couldn't help but whimper.

He slid his palm lower, between my legs, bunching the fabric of my nightgown.

I so needed this.

He licked along the shell of my ear, sending goosebumps all over my body. "Don't you have an answer for me?"

If I denied his words, he'd know I lied. I fucking craved him with every ounce of my being, and I hated him for it. The feel of him, his touch, the way he smelled, his presence. He fucked with my head in a way no one else had.

I'd become addicted.

"This is temporary. Your terms"—I dropped one hand from the bar, threading my fingers into the strands of his hair—"for my freedom. Wasn't that what you said?"

He slowly exposed the skin along my legs, until he reached my hips. "You do hate this life, don't you, Nyx?"

"I love my family." I closed my eyes and arched as his mouth glided from my throat to the valley of my breasts, and the fingers of one hand pushed beneath my underwear, finding my soaked pussy.

"That's not what I asked you." He teased my swollen clit, circling, strumming, flicking. "What makes you hate it so much?"

"I'm a pawn in everyone else's game. Including yours, including your family's."

He jerked my thong from my hips, letting it slide down my legs, and without thought, I stepped out of it, kicking it to the side. The next thing I heard was the slide of his belt, and immediately, my pussy contracted, desperate for the thick thrust of his cock inside me.

"But my games, you like very much." He released his hold on me. "Give me your wrists."

When I followed his directions and saw the feral lust in his dark eyes, I felt as if I were staring at some Greek god about to ravish me.

Fuck. This man had my body igniting into an inferno of flames with one look or touch, and he pushed at parts of me I couldn't afford to set free without leading to complete heartache.

This was temporary, I had to remember. His path lay riddled with chains.

He lifted my arms, wrapping my fingers back around the metal, and then bound my wrists to the thick bars of the trellis.

Stepping back, he licked his lips and then brushed his thumb over mine. "You're the queen in this game, Goddess. Haven't you figured it out? That's why people like Camilla are scared of you. Why they give you such a hard time."

"I'm the anomaly no one can make sense of."

He pulled his shirt over his head, tossing it to the ground, and then unbuttoned his jeans to free his beautiful weeping erection. He gathered my nightgown around my waist and lifted my legs around his hips.

"This is going to be hard and fast. You with me?"

"Simon, I'm always with you. You know how I like it."

Just as he slid his thick cock through my slick pussy lips and aligned it to my sopping entrance, he asked, "Would it be so bad to marry me?"

A lump formed in my throat, and a pressure built in my heart as I stared into his intense emerald eyes.

"Yes," I whispered, feeling the burn of his question deep in my heart. "You'd want me to be someone I'm not."

Something like hurt flashed across his gorgeous face, right before he slammed into me, making me gasp and arch up.

"Simon."

"Is that what you believe or what you want to believe?" He pulled out to the tip and drove back in.

I arched up into him, needing the friction of each thrust of his pelvis. "Does it matter? We want different things."

"Do we?"

He fucked me hard, not letting up his pace. Something shifted between us, something I couldn't let matter.

"Open your eyes," he ordered, making me realize I'd tried to block out everything but the sensations coursing inside my body.

We held each other's gazes as he pistoned in and out of me, his breath unsteady, face flushed, pupils so dilated they looked black. The pain of the bars digging into my back was a wicked pleasure I couldn't understand why I enjoyed so much. Every thrust and shift of his hips hit spots only he'd ever known and drove my need higher.

"Please," I begged. "I need."

"That's right. Beg for it."

I writhed, thrashing and jerking my bound arms. "Please, Simon, let me come."

Pressing my heels into his ass, I tried to pull him closer to give me the extra friction I needed to go over.

He released one of my hips, gliding his palm up the side of my body until he fisted my hair and tugged my head back.

"Is this what you want?" He rolled his hips in the exact way I needed.

My vaginal walls quivered and contracted. "Yes, harder. You know I need it harder."

"If I fuck you the way you want, your family is going to hear you." He brought his mouth to mine, nipping my lower lip as his thrusts grew harder. "Hear me fucking you. Hear you begging for it. They're going to know you're not the innocent they think you are. They're going to know I corrupted you. They're going to know your pussy curves to my cock. Then you won't have a choice."

I gasped as my pussy clamped down on his thick shaft. "Stop saying shit like that and just fuck me. I'm not the woman you want to marry. That role belongs to someone like that bitch Camilla."

"I get to decide who the role belongs to, not you." His pounding grew brutal and brought me higher and higher toward the peak I was so desperate to go over. "Your future is in my hands."

"We both know I'd make a terrible wife. I don't fit the mold. I'll give you too much trouble. Besides, you promised."

His green eyes bore into mine for a split second, and he nodded and then muttered, "You could always take the promise back."

That was when he hit the bundle of nerves deep inside me, and I detonated. Simon's mouth covered mine, muffling my cry. My pussy quivered and contracted around his cock, ecstasy washing through every part of my body.

He continued to fuck into me. His hold in my hair a tight vise grip, while the fingers of his other hand dug into my hips and ass. His breath grew ragged, and he grew thicker and harder. Seconds later, he exploded, gritting his teeth with my name on his lips.

17

SIMON

"WE NEED TO HAVE A CHAT, DRAKOS," WERE THE FIRST WORDS I heard as I entered the Ida Resort and Casino.

Hagen Lykaios stood before me, a scowl on his face that told me he either wanted to beat the shit out of me or kill me.

Which one? I wasn't sure.

The fucking last thing I wanted to do was have another complication stand between me and Nyx. Since I'd returned from Greece, every time I turned around, the universe kept finding some obstacle or another to throw in my way to make sure I spent as little time as possible with her.

First, it was more trouble with suppliers for my ship build-outs, then it was continuous weeding of the shits trying to undermine my business.

All I wanted was a fucking break.

Now here was her overprotective cousin to give me some lecture.

The man was six-foot-three with a brawler build and would have intimidated the fuck out of anyone who hadn't been raised by an equally scary motherfucker.

The fact Penny Lykaios, a pixie-sized woman who barely passed five-foot-two, could marry him and hold her own was a testimony to her strength and will. According to Nyx, Penny ran the Lykaios household, even if Hagen acted like he controlled things.

"Lykaios," I greeted him and then replied, "I have other matters to see to first."

Like the goddess who was waiting for me in her bathtub.

The picture she'd sent me a few seconds before I'd walked inside the doors of the hotel was burning a hole in my pocket.

"It can wait."

I lifted a brow. "I'm not one of the regular chumps you can order about."

"And I own this resort. You want to get anywhere near my baby cousin, I suggest you take a moment to have a chat with me." Hagen smirked. "Or would you rather this conversation happens with her brothers? In my opinion, I'm the lesser of the two evils."

I held his gaze, not saying anything for a moment, then nodded. "You get ten minutes."

"Let's go." Hagen turned and then moved in the direction of the casino.

"Does Nyx know you're taking on the role of protective big brother?" I asked as my security team and I followed Hagen into the casino.

"That's up to you to tell her. She is your fiancée." Hagen nodded to an attendant who stood guard near a series of glass panels.

The man inclined his head and waved a key card across the seam between two sections. A false wall popped open to reveal a hallway leading into a giant reception area with offices in the back.

This place was modern and fancy as fuck. And the technology made the space look more like a center for an IT company than a resort and casino's central hub.

"Let's go into my office. This way we have privacy." Once inside, Hagen offered, "Want a drink?"

"No, I'm good. I'd rather you get to the point."

"Have it your way."

We took our seats in a lounge-type setup by a bay of windows giving views of a curated outdoor garden with strategically placed fountains and lights. It gave the illusion of being an outdoor greenhouse nightclub, without the loud music or enclosure.

Once seated, Hagen leaned forward and glared at me. "I know you're sleeping with her. Does this mean you're planning to go through with the wedding?"

Well, that was direct.

Then again, I wouldn't expect anything less from Draco's former enforcer. The man had a reputation for no bullshit.

Hagen was related to Nyx's mother, so I wondered why he hadn't divulged my relationship with Nyx to her family. Maybe it was a courtesy to Draco or to Nyx—possibly a bit of both.

"I won't force her."

Well, maybe I would, but I wasn't going to tell him.

Who was I kidding? No one could force Nyx to do any damn thing.

"That's not what I asked you."

"It's her decision."

"Does this mean you'd let her go if she said no?"

My stomach clenched at the mere idea, but I kept my face as emotionless as possible. "I'd do everything in my power to convince her otherwise."

Hagen smirked. "Good luck with that. She isn't someone who is easily swayed."

"I know this better than you believe. She is singular when it comes to her plans."

"Then let me give you this piece of advice."

I waited for him to finish.

"Do what my Starlight did for me. She accepted me the way I am. She knew my past and understood there were aspects of my life that would stay tied to it."

The syndicate, he meant.

Nyx was born into and spoke of leaving the world, whereas Penny had chosen to step inside it.

"I don't want her to change." I held Hagen's cool blue gaze. "And I've never asked her to change."

"What about that perfect debutante you were rumored to have selected for yourself prior to the engagement? From what I heard, she met everything on your checklist, and it was almost a done deal until your uncle decided to throw a monkey wrench in your plans."

I looked back to my original plans and how I'd expected my life to unfold. Camilla came from the right background, had the social connections, and knew the rules. She would have made the perfect wife.

But the thought of being with anyone like her after all this time with Nyx was like choosing between a life of restrictions and obligations and one filled with laughter and freedom.

Freedom.

Was this how Nyx felt? Was this the reason she wanted to leave so desperately? Why she had chosen Vegas?

God, could I make her choose me?

A better man would say no.

Fuck.

I couldn't let her go.

"I accept Nyx the way she is. It's better to have someone who can stab a man in the gut than someone who needs rescuing all the time."

"Then all I have to say is, good luck." Hagen rose from his seat. "You're going to need it. One Mykos is a challenge to face —you have a whole family to contend with."

FIFTEEN MINUTES AFTER LEAVING HAGEN, I ARRIVED AT NYX'S penthouse in the Ida residential tower.

Tony and Stevie stood outside her door. Both spoke to each other as if trying to make a decision. They rarely took shifts patrolling Nyx's floor together. If one worked, the other took that shift off. Nyx's game nights were the only exception, and the next one wasn't for another month.

Stevie clenched her jaw, released a sigh, and then nodded.

Okay, this was interesting.

Both of them retrained their attention to me and came toward me.

The fuck?

How many people were going to cockblock me in this damn hotel?

"We would like a word." Stevie adjusted her stance in that way she always moved when she meant business.

Normally, I'd have said something to annoy the former champion mixed martial artist, but whatever these two had to tell me gave me the sense Nyx probably didn't want me to know about it.

"Did something happen?" I asked.

"You could say that." Stevie pulled out her phone, then showed me a video from hotel ceiling surveillance footage.

It showed me a picture of Hal in the botanical gardens pacing and flipping what looked like a poker chip from a Silent Night game between his fingers.

In the far distance, I could see Nyx coming out from the employee side of the botanical gardens.

How the fuck had he gotten one of those chips?

From the second Nyx had mentioned the other Drakos on the day I'd flown back from Greece, I'd known it was Hal. No one else wanted to fuck with me or go after anyone who I viewed as mine.

Albert hated me on the principle of standing in the way of the family legacy. I had no doubt if I'd been the son of a younger brother, he wouldn't have given me a second thought. However, Hal was a completely different story. The fucker hated me even before my parents' deaths. We were only a few months apart in age, and I couldn't remember a time when something wasn't a competition.

Maybe it was Gio's fault for expecting perfection out of his grandsons.

No, that wasn't the only reason. Hal took things to an extreme level. From the way we dressed and going after the same girls in high school, to pursuing the same degree in college. He had to do everything bigger, badder, better.

Now, he was at it again.

Stevie turned to the next reel.

This one had Hal at a distance but Nyx front and center. Her recognizing him, then turning, pausing to call someone, and then Tony arriving.

Why the fuck hadn't she told me about this? We talked every damn day. She was in so much trouble.

I lifted my head. "I've seen enough."

"We haven't even gotten close. This is from one of the people I had tailing him. I thought it better not to get the Lykaioses involved and have to explain why I needed footage of anyone other than Nyx."

She flipped again.

This video showed Hal's anger when Nyx hadn't shown up, and then the footage pieced together following him through the hotel up until he reached the residential tower, where security turned him away.

"You need to handle this." Tony moved in next to Stevie. "I've watched over her since she was born, and I won't have her become a pawn in this war you're planning with your family."

I remained quiet for a few seconds, staring at the screen. All of a sudden, I noticed the date and time.

This wasn't recent, but a fucking month ago. I clenched my jaw.

She'd told me she never met with the other Drakos. She may have not lied, but she'd known who he was and the significance of what he held, and she'd kept it from me. Why would she hide this from me?

We'd come so far in this thing between us, and she still refused to give me a goddamned inch.

Hal wouldn't hesitate to use any means necessary to ruin her reputation or destroy her, if it meant paving the way for him in the family.

I was the one damn person who could protect her from him. Hell, his body language showed he was scared shitless of getting caught.

Why couldn't she trust me?

If only she'd trusted me, I would have had that damn chip in my hand now.

Pushing down the riot of emotions bubbling inside me, I asked, "Want to explain to me why no one saw fit to tell me about this?"

"You know now," Stevie responded.

"Bullshit. What happened?"

"This arrived." Tony handed me a small package.

Inside was the poker chip from one of Nyx's game nights and a photograph of a younger Nyx with David, and on the table behind them were the same chips. It looked as if Nyx wasn't even aware the picture was taken. And from what I knew of her games, all electronics were confiscated at entry.

She'd trusted this shithead. He was her friend, and he'd fucked her over.

"There's a note, as well."

You shouldn't have stood me up. What would your fiancé do if he knew about your activities? Let's negotiate.

    H

Rage filled my gut, and it took all my effort not to call in the order to take them all out. He wanted to use Nyx for some bigger purpose.

Over my dead body.

No.

Over *his* fucking dead body.

I'd kill him before he touched her.

I lifted my gaze to Stevie and Tony. "Has she seen this?"

"Not yet. It arrived an hour ago. With the increased security, we open all boxes addressed to her," Stevie answered.

"I'm adding my people to yours."

"She's going to give you hell. Especially since we already doubled her protection."

"I have no doubt, but she'll live with it."

"Good luck handling that situation."

The smirk on Stevie's face told me she thought I was in for it with Nyx, but she had no idea how pissed I was at the moment.

I grabbed the chip and moved toward her door. "Oh, I'm about to handle it."

Stepping inside her apartment, I unbuttoned and shrugged

off my jacket, throwing it on the back of the sectional in Nyx's living room as I made my way to her bedroom.

The door sat half ajar, and the music from her favorite satellite radio station played. I stepped inside. The scents of lavender and eucalyptus lingered in the air, and a towel lay draped over the arm of a chair.

Looking inside the bathroom, I couldn't help but shake my head at the enormous tub taking center stage.

The woman loved her long baths, and apparently, that meant she needed something big enough to accommodate five people. Until her, I'd never spent any time lounging inside a tub. I'd viewed it as a waste of time.

Shower and get to work. More efficient.

Now, I enjoyed the fuck out them, specifically with a wet, naked Nyx to slide balls-deep into.

Which I missed doing because of all the interruptions.

Which brought me back to my mission.

Making sure Nyx never kept something from me again, especially when it came to her safety.

I scanned the balcony through the open windows and noticed Nyx wearing a robe and leaning against a half-wall railing drinking a glass of wine. Behind her on a table, another one.

She was so fucking beautiful. The lights of the Vegas Strip below her gave her an otherworldly glow.

Grabbing hold of the belt of her robe, she untied it and tossed the silk behind her, revealing a barely there piece of lingerie that exposed more than it covered.

Immediately, my cock jumped, and for a split second, I wanted to change my mind about the plans I had for her.

Maybe, if I could get her compliance to my terms, then I'd reconsider.

I was so full of it. I knew damn well come morning I'd have fucked her raw.

Her attention shifted to me as I moved through the bedroom access to her terrace.

A line formed between her brows, and she cocked her head to the side as if she sensed something wasn't quite right.

"What's wrong?"

Taking the chip out of my pocket, I spun it on its edge on the table.

"You tell me."

18

NYX

OH, DEAR GOD. I COULDN'T BELIEVE WHAT I WAS SEEING. THE
last time I saw that chip, it was in Hal's hand, and now it spun
in a circular dance on my patio table.

And from the cool, emotionless green stare Simon was
shooting at me, I was in so much fucking trouble.

"H-how?"

"How is this in my possession?" He smacked his hand over
the round disk and moved in my direction, making my
heartbeat accelerate. "It came in a package for you today, with a
picture of you from your college years."

"That's not possible." I shook my head.

No fucking way. I had people frisked before events. Even
now, I made sure everyone went through an electronic scan.

He nodded, getting closer to me. "Your old friend David took a picture of you at one of your games."

Motherfucker. How the hell could he have gotten something through? I closed my eyes for a few seconds, trying to wrack my brain for when it could have happened.

Then I remembered the party where he'd subbed in at the last minute. He'd arrived right before play. Like an idiot, I believed him when I asked if he'd dropped his key and phone in the front bin.

He was a liar from the beginning.

Clenching my jaw, I gritted out, "I really hate that guy."

"I'll take care of that situation. At this point in time, I need to attend to another one."

My breath grew unsteady, and I took a step back in retreat. And for some illogical reason, the fact he was this level of angry and prowling in my direction had my nipples beading and clit throbbing.

"What situation?" I asked, knowing damn well he meant me.

When he was right upon me, he set his palms on my waist and pushed me back against the terrace wall.

"The situation where the woman in my life decided not to tell me an enemy of mine had something that could hurt her." He leaned in until his face was a hairsbreadth from mine. "Something that could have significant consequences for her and her family if made public."

He reached up and gripped my jaw, biting my lower lip hard enough to give a delicious sting. Pleasure-pain coursed deep into my pussy, and my cleft grew slick with arousal.

Why the fuck did I like it so much when he went all aggressive like that?

"Something that would push people to tell me to end what I have with her."

My desire cooled as I focused on the last part of his list, and a lump formed deep in my gut.

I wasn't ready for this to end. I still had nine more months.

Oh God, what was happening to me? The thought of us going our separate ways wasn't supposed to hurt like this.

I swallowed, trying to relieve the burning in the back of my throat, and whispered, "I'm sorry."

"Oh, you're going to be sorry." He spun me around to face the city. "Hands on the edge of the balcony and don't move them."

"S-Simon..." My voice shook, revealing the uncertainty coursing through me.

"Remember when I told you I will do what I want, whenever I want, however I want?"

"Yes."

"Well, this is one of those times."

"What are you going to do?"

He wrapped my hair around one fist and then pushed his aroused body against my back, sandwiching me between him and the balcony half wall. "You will just have to find out."

The ache deep in my core ignited into a racing fire as my breasts grew heavy and full.

He ran the stubble of his beard along the column of my throat, stopping at that spot that sent me to exquisite bliss. Instead of licking and sucking as I expected, he bypassed the juncture of my neck and shoulder.

I couldn't help but whimper, flexing my fingers on the stone. "Simon."

He lifted his piercing green gaze to mine, a slight curve to his lips telling me he'd wanted that very reaction.

Bastard.

He slid the palm of his free hand up my stomach, cupping my breast through the material of my teddy and then pinching my nipple in an almost too-painful hold, making me gasp.

A shiver slid down my spine, as my vaginal muscles quickened and spasmed.

"You love the edge of pain, don't you, Goddess?" he asked as he moved to the other breast, giving it the same beautiful torture.

I closed my eyes, losing myself in the endorphins filling my system. "I didn't know I did until you."

"That's right. This body belongs to me." His palm glided down my torso until he reached the hem of silk that barely covered my thighs.

Reaching underneath, he grabbed the front of my thong, and before I could tell him to stop, with a hard jerk, he ripped it from my hips.

"Are you crazy? This set was expensive."

"Ask me if I care." He slid two fingers between the folds of my wet, swollen pussy lips, trapping my clit between his knuckles.

Oh God. My legs grew weak, knowing what was coming and finally figuring out his game.

He planned to torture me with sex.

"You see," he continued as he gradually increased the pressure of the digits holding my clitoral nub hostage, "my woman didn't give a shit what it could have cost her if that bastard got his hands on her."

"Am I your woman?"

In the next second, I cried out as white-hot pleasure-filled pain shot into my system. My breath locked in my chest, and my legs gave out, leaving Simon's body the only reason I stayed upright. When he finally released my pulsing bundle of nerves, I sighed in relief and almost begged him to do it again.

"Ask me that again." The angry edge to his voice surprised me.

Knowing better than to do as he ordered, I asked, "Does this mean you're my man?"

He thrust his two fingers deep into my soaked pussy and then spoke into my ear. "I'm the fucking darkness to your night."

He pumped in and out of me, hitting all the right places inside me. My core contracted and flooded his hand.

"I'm the master of your future," he continued.

His rhythm shifted and then slowed, bringing me down from the climb to the peak I strived to reach.

"I'm your master of fortune."

He changed his tempo again, driving up my need again, this time curving his fingers and ratcheting my arousal higher and higher. And just like before, right when I was about to shatter, he brought me back down.

"Dammit, Simon. Let me come," I shouted.

"No."

"Asshole."

"Never denied it." He jerked my head back with my hair again, lust burning in his emerald depths. "And I'm the asshole whose cock you claimed as yours."

He brought his mouth down on mine and began to piston

his fingers again. The taste of him, his anger, his desire heightened my need.

He repeated the agony of bringing me to the cusp then letting me fall to nothing, three more times.

"Simon, please," I begged, unable to take it anymore.

"No." He added a third finger and then worried my tender clit. "Only my woman deserves to come."

Barely able to breathe, my mind clouded. "I'm your fucking woman. You know this."

"Do I? Because that means you would tell me when shit happens. Trust me when shit happens."

He pulled free of my body and untangled his fingers from my hair, taking a step back.

I turned to face him.

We stared at each other for a few seconds. That's when I saw the tinge of sadness in his jeweled eyes that rarely gave anything away.

Oh fuck, I'd hurt his feelings.

This man, who the world at large believed possessed no emotions or heart, seemed to feel more than anyone realized.

Me, especially. Maybe this wasn't one-sided, after all.

"I'm sorry." I reached up to cup his cheek, but he clasped his fingers around my wrist.

"You will not compromise your safety again."

"I should have said something to you."

His other hand gripped my waist and then tugged me to him.

"I never met with him." I sighed. "But I hear you."

"Now we need to establish something else."

"What is that?"

"Whether or not anyone outside of our people knows, we are together."

A tremor shook my heart.

"Simon, we have an end date."

A frown marred his face as if he wanted to argue. "End date or not, we are a couple. Is that clear?"

I swallowed, knowing this road could only lead to heartache later but unable to do anything but accept what was happening to me.

I nodded. "For the rest of this year, we are together."

Pushing down the pain my words ignited, I set a hand on his shoulder and rose up onto tiptoes, bringing my lips flush to his.

At first, he resisted, then something snapped. His mouth took over as he released my wrist and slid his palms up to the front of my teddy, grabbed hold of the material, and tore the delicate fabric down the front.

I gasped, breaking the kiss.

The almost violent, feral lust staring back at me should have scared me. Instead, it shot a spasm deep into my core and drove the unsatisfied ache to come even higher.

This man was too gorgeous for his own good and possessed this ability to bring out a side of me I'd never known existed.

He tossed my very expensive rag to the ground before grabbing hold of my waist again and walking me backward until my ass pressed against the half wall balcony of my terrace.

"Turn around. I'm going to fuck you while the city watches." The seriousness of his gaze told me he wasn't joking.

Holy fuck. We were really going to do this.

Yes, he'd just finger-fucked me to frustration hell and back, but the half wall covered the lower part of my body. And only the people who lived at a higher level in the tower across from mine could chance seeing Simon's hand between my legs.

With me naked and Simon behind me, no one could doubt what activities were taking place on this balcony.

And for some crazy reason, this whole idea aroused the hell out of me.

"Goddess, I gave you an order."

Goosebumps prickled my skin, and my breath came out in unsteady pants.

God, I loved when his voice went all gravelly like that.

I followed his instructions, wrapping my fingers around the edge of the concrete half wall.

When he stepped up behind me, I felt him fully clothed, and a nudge of disappointment settled on my shoulders. I loved the feel of him, skin to skin, and he knew it.

"Simon?" I questioned through ragged breaths.

"All you get is my cock. You hold back, I hold back."

Well, shit. He was still mad.

I heard the sound of his zipper lowering and then the steel length of his thick cock nestled along the hollow of my back.

He kicked my feet slightly apart and then slid the smooth, bulbous head of his shaft along the slick lips of my pussy. He rubbed back and forth, making sure to nudge my oversensitized clit with each pass.

I closed my eyes, reveling in the hypnotic torment.

Then, all of a sudden, he slammed into me.

"Oh God. Simon," I called, completely sandwiched between him and the wall.

The abrasiveness of his zipper on my ass with the feel of his thick, hard length deep in me was a heady combination of both pleasure and pain.

He wanted me to feel the discomfort, the knowledge there was a barrier between us.

The hurt I'd seen in his eyes earlier flashed in my mind, making me realize something. This whole thing was about trust.

He'd said those words, and now it had finally sunk in. He wanted my full trust.

I trusted him with my body, to do things that pushed conventional boundaries right and left. Though, when it came to the situation with his cousin, I'd kept it to myself. He'd taken it as a matter of trust, not believing he could handle it.

This relationship thing was complicated.

He pulled out to the tip and thrust back in, starting a smooth, steady tempo meant to build my need slowly, making it almost impossible for me to come without his help.

My punishment definitely wasn't over.

My pussy wept with need, soaking his cock with each pass in and out, and my breasts ached.

Without realizing it, I whimpered, "Need more."

"I know you do," he answered between breaths. "So do I."

He cupped my throat and jaw, angling my chin. I peered into his dark, desire-glazed green eyes.

I couldn't be seeing what I thought I was seeing.

The burning I'd felt in my throat the night in my greenhouse returned, and I bit my lower lip to keep it from trembling.

He rubbed his thumb over my mouth and then, at the same time, shifted his pace. My pussy quivered first in tiny spasms and then ripples, and the pleasure rising in my body overtook me.

"Oh, Simon," I moaned, unable to do anything but leverage myself against the wall and take the force of each of his thrusts. "I'm almost there."

"You're mine, Goddess. I protect what's mine. You have to trust me."

"I do."

"Are you mine?"

The intensity in his irises pushed my emotions into a tailspin.

"Y-y-yes. I'm yours."

As if that was what he was wanting to hear, his mouth covered mine in a hungry kiss. He rolled his hips in that perfect way to rub that spot deep inside me, and I detonated.

I cried out, clenching my eyes tight. My pussy clamped down on the girth of his pistoning cock, and utter relief from the wicked torture washed through my system.

My fingers clutched on the arm Simon braced around my waist, and I knew if he wasn't holding me to him, I would have fallen to the floor. The pleasure cascading through me was too much.

"Fuck. You're squeezing me so tight."

I couldn't respond as the muscles of my sex continued to flex in unending, rhythmic waves, stealing all my breath.

As my orgasm waned, he pushed me forward and then set an intense, brutal pace meant for him. But as usual, the more aggressive his hold on my hips and his thrusts became, the more I wanted this side of him.

My pussy contracted, and a hiss escaped Simon's lips. "Definitely mine."

He pumped in and out, keeping with the hard, unrelenting thrusts. My body, so primed from my earlier release, exploded. Ecstasy washed over me, while my sex fisted Simon's thick, hard cock.

Not a second later, I heard, "Fuck, fuck, fuck," as Simon came deep inside me.

We both rode out our orgasms, gasping and moaning. Loud, uncaring if anyone could hear us.

Lifting my face to the night sky, I gulped in air and accepted the damn truth.

I was in love with the asshole behind me.

19

SIMON

"ARE YOU MEETING WITH HIM, OR ARE YOU LETTING HIM HANG IN the wind?" Kasen asked me as I made my way through the luxury high-rise where Nyx was in the middle of one of her Silent Night events.

"I'm going. Santos thinks I don't know he's working with Albert."

The fucker thought he could play both sides, acting as if he was an ally, all the while poising himself as a second to Albert and Hal.

After the incident with Camilla and Nyx, I'd wanted anything and everything on Camilla and her father. It was interesting how much information one could acquire from those burned by a person claiming to be a friend and turning on them. Apparently, Camilla had left a trail of them over her twenty-seven years.

The investigation also uncovered Kes Santos's multiple trips out of the country, one of them happening to be Thessaloniki, where I'd spent that fucking month renegotiating contracts with multiple shipping partners.

I had no doubt he'd played the middleman for many of my problems.

"He's attached himself to your idiot cousin. I'm assuming he's trying to pawn his daughter onto him."

I shrugged. "Good luck to him."

"I take it you're no longer interested in the debutante."

"Hal can have her. I have a goddess."

Kasen pushed the button for the private elevator accessing the penthouse, lifting his gaze to the camera. When the doors opened, we stepped inside.

As the cab started its ascent, Kasen shook his head. "Do you understand the shit you're about to start if you do what I think you're going to do?"

"I'm not starting anything. I'm finishing something."

"They're going to view it as you stole her and broke a deal."

"It's not breaking anything if she picks me."

"And you're positive she'll pick you? Especially after how adamant she was about leaving this life?"

I thought about how things had changed between us since that night on her terrace a month ago. Hell, the change had started in the greenhouse in the Hamptons.

She knew as much about me as I knew about her. It was as if we could let down our guards with each other.

"She'll pick me."

I hoped, anyway.

If she hesitated, I'd get her to see there was no escaping the life. She lived an underground existence, even here in Vegas.

A fucking botanist by day and illegal high-stakes poker organizer by night.

Nothing was normal in her world, no matter what she believed. She'd created an illusion of the life she could lead, and she knew it.

If she were my woman, I could protect her. No one would dare touch her.

I'd kill them with my bare hands.

Which put Hal on the top of the list for even threatening anything against her.

"No matter her decision, you'll need to deal with the men in her life. You have a contract. You'd give up the port for her?"

The elevator stopped, and the doors opened.

"In a heartbeat," I answered, stepping out into the penthouse.

"You never fucking make anything easy, do you? I'll assemble the cleanup team for the carnage when the Surgeon gets his hands on you."

"Asshole," I muttered and walked into the gaming room, coming to an abrupt halt and narrowing my gaze. "Who the fuck is that?"

Some fucker had his hand on Nyx's waist, whispering something in her ear.

She laughed, throwing back her head. Other people around her joined in on the merriment. Then the jerk ran a hand down her back as if he had a right to touch her.

"Since we just got here, I have no idea." Kasen grabbed my shoulder. "Let's not kill anyone."

Stevie approached, a smirk on her face. "Don't get your panties in a twist. He flirts with everyone. He's harmless."

"That is more than flirting."

"He must have forgotten the cardinal rule of never flirt with a mobster's fiancée. Oh, wait. You build ships, right?"

I gave her a cool stare, the one that scared the shit out of most people. However, it seemed to have as little effect on her as it did on Nyx.

"I prefer syndicate. And my main business is shipping." I pushed Kasen's hand from my chest and moved in Nyx's direction.

As I neared, her attention shifted, completely focusing on me. The smile on her lips at seeing me should have soothed the irritation prickling at the back of my mind, but my annoyance remained.

"Hi. You're late."

I offered her my hand. "Come with me. I'd like a private word with you."

A line formed between her brows, but she slid a palm over mine. "Is everything okay?"

"It will be. Which way to the primary bedroom?"

"Down the hall and to the left."

Stopping at the glass door of the over-the-top modern room, I instructed, "When we go in there, don't say a word. Just do as I say."

Her breath hitched, and she glanced up at my face. "Here?"

"Not a word." I turned the knob, and we stepped in.

I pushed the button to tint the walls of the glass-enclosed bedroom before locking it to make sure no one could disturb us.

She stared at me with her dark eyes. Her breath instantly grew shallow, and a flush crept up her cheeks.

Setting my hands on her hips, I walked her backward until I had her crowded against the bench ledge of the window overlooking the Vegas skyline and Strip.

This place was truly a voyeur's dream with the idea of wanting people to see in as well as look outward. Windows made up most of the walls of the suite with the exception of those encompassing the bathrooms.

This was definitely something Nyx would enjoy, especially after that night a month ago on her terrace.

However, right now, I wanted to make a point to my fiancée, and it would happen without the possibility of any spectators.

"Si—"

I cut her off, pressing my thumb against her mouth.

"I said, not a word."

She gripped my forearms as a haze of lust filled her onyx gaze, and a light flush appeared on her cheeks.

I slid my palm down her neck to cup her throat, giving it a slight squeeze, and watched her pupils dilate. She licked her plump lips, giving me visions of the way she looked up at me as she deep-throated my cock.

My dick swelled rock-hard in my pants, making me want to grit my teeth.

Yeah, that was definitely on the menu for later.

Leaning forward, I kissed her. First, with gentle passes over her plump lips, then deepening the embrace, tasting her, savoring her, drowning in her.

God, this woman made me crave her, day and night.

When she pulled back, a wicked smile tugged at the corner of her mouth.

And it was as if she'd read my thoughts from only a moment earlier. She reversed our positions, pressing me back, and then dropped to her knees.

"Fuck, Goddess."

"Shhh. You said no talking." Her fingers went to work on my belt, pulling the leather free from its confines before she moved on to the fastening of my pants.

The whole time, she petted and stroked me through the material of my slacks.

By the time she freed my hard, aching cock, I was ready to grab the back of her head and lose myself down her throat.

The witch was prolonging it to torture me.

"Remember, payback is a bitch." I slid my fingers under her thick hair and gripped the back of her neck.

She fisted my cock, up and down, and then squeezed the base right before she leaned forward and licked the precum beading at the tip.

"Promises, promises," she hummed, a wicked glint in her gaze.

"Goddess, my cock better be in—" I threw my head back as she engulfed me, taking me deep and letting me hit the back of her throat, right before she swallowed.

Fuck, I loved when she did that.

I circled my fingers into her hair, trying my hardest to let her control the pace. She bobbed up and down, licking and stroking the vein under my cock.

She worked me just as I liked.

She was perfect.

My breath grew ragged as my need drove higher, and I felt the familiar urge to shift her rhythm, fuck her harder, grip her hair, and claim her mouth. Instead, I pulled free of her and brought her to her feet.

Turning her, I lifted her onto the ledge. Reaching under her dress, I gripped the sides of her underwear and slid them over her hips. Once I had her thong free of her body, I threw it on a nearby chair.

Cupping her sex, I found her soaked. She closed her eyes and moaned, arching her throat. Leaning forward, I bit the juncture of where her shoulder and neck met, giving her the sting she loved.

I pushed my pants completely down, gripped her hips as I stepped between her legs, and in the next second, thrust into her heat.

"Simon," she cried out.

I set a relentless pace, fucking her with the intensity of the need she'd built with her mouth and the desire I'd felt to mark her from the moment I saw that asshole flirting with her.

Her fingers dug into my shoulders and mine dug into her hips.

Neither of us spoke as we held each other's gazes. Emotions swirled in her eyes, and now I knew there was no fucking way I'd give up this woman.

She was mine. Consequences be damned.

Gio Drakos had failed. I wasn't like him.

My father hadn't failed my family by marrying my mother. Gio had failed my father by not accepting my mother.

Nyx fucking made me *feel*. How the hell had that happened?

Gliding my palm up her body, I fisted her hair, tilted her

head back, and stared into her onyx eyes. "You're mine. Do you understand this?"

"This is jus—"

"Don't lie, Nyx." A whimper escaped her mouth as I tightened my grip on her hair and adjusted my thrusts. "I see it in your eyes. I've seen it in your eyes since the night in your greenhouse."

Her lips trembled, and she closed her lids for a brief moment. "What do you think you see?"

"That you know you're mine. That you belong to me. That I'm going to keep you." I shifted my hand on her hip and used my thumb to stroke her swollen clit, causing her to buck into each pump of my cock.

"Oh God," she cried out. "I…I won't let you trap me."

"Is it a trap when you want me to keep you?" I leaned down, biting her swollen lower lip before freeing my grip from her hair and repositioning my hold onto her hips.

"Simon, don't say things like that. It scares me, confuses me, makes me want things I shouldn't."

At least I wasn't the only one having these thoughts.

Stopping the movement of my hips, I dared, "Tell me you don't feel it every time we're apart. Or when we're together. Tell me you can walk away."

She swallowed and remained quiet for a few seconds, a play of emotions cascading over her face.

When she finally spoke, she said, "Can we discuss this after you finish fucking me? I can't think."

She dug her nails into the skin at the back of my neck and pressed her heels against my thighs, trying to urge me to follow her request.

I held her dark passion-filled gaze, knowing she had no clue about the storm raging inside me or the fact she'd become a part of my life I wasn't sure I could live without.

Releasing a deep breath, I pushed my warring thoughts to the back of my mind and focused on the beautiful woman in my arms.

"Are you saying you want me to shut up and fuck you?"

"Exactly."

"Your wish is my command." I wrapped my arm around her waist, pulled my cock out to the tip, and thrust forward into her dripping pussy.

"Yes," she gasped, throwing her head back. "Like that."

She released her hold on my neck and braced one hand on the ledge behind her, pushing against it to give her the leverage she needed to meet each of my thrusts.

This woman was unlike anything I ever expected. How the hell had she gotten so deep under my skin?

"I'm almost there. Oh God." Her pussy quivered and then clamped down, flooding my cock with arousal.

"That's it, come for me." I rolled my hips in the way it would completely send her over, and, almost immediately, she shattered.

"Simon," she cried out, body bowing, nails raking my shoulders, and pussy fisting my cock in a vise grip.

Fucking gorgeous.

There was nothing like the beauty of her going over.

Each spasm of her pussy drove at my own need to come, but I wasn't ready for this to end.

"One more," I commanded as I threaded my fingers into her hair and drew her mouth to mine.

"I don't think I can."

"Of course, you can," I murmured against her lips a second before I pulled out and slammed back in, making both of us gasp.

Neither of us spoke any more words as our bodies took over and filled the room with the sounds of sex.

When she came a second time, I followed almost immediately after her, clutching her to me and knowing I'd done the very thing Pappous told me never to do.

Gave the world a weakness to use against me.

Except I would burn everything and everyone to the ground to protect her. And, unlike my father, I had the power to do it.

20

SIMON

"WANT TO TELL ME WHAT THIS WAS ALL ABOUT?" NYX ASKED AS my cock softened inside her and I tried to catch my breath.

I continued to hold her against me and remained quiet for a few seconds, unsure of how to clearly say my words without sounding like a Neanderthal.

Finally, after gathering my thoughts, I said, "No one touches what's mine. Is that clear?"

She lifted her head, a frown marring her beautiful flushed face. "This is about Dustin flirting with me. Are you serious?"

"As a heart attack."

"I still don't understand."

"When you're walking around your poker room tonight and some fucker decides he wants to make a play for you, you need to remember a few things."

"Such as?"

"You need to remember who just came inside you. Whose cum just marked you, who you belong to."

"Was this all about jealousy? About marking your territory?"

My hold on her scalp tightened as I shifted, slipping from her body. "You know damn well it's more. There's no ending this."

"Simon, don't say things you don't mean." She bit her lip in that way she would do when she tried to hold in her emotions. "There is too much on the line."

She pushed at my chest, and I released her, letting her move away from me. The panic on her face told me she had a war raging inside her. If only she could understand the same roller coaster raged inside me. The same fear, the same worries, the same needs.

The woman fucking made me want shit I never even thought to have with anyone else. I resisted the impulse to touch her—it would only make her run, with the panic I saw bubbling up inside her.

Instead of making any comment, I dressed and moved to lean against the glass outer wall of the room

All of a sudden, she glanced down between her legs and then shot me a glare over her shoulder.

I shouldn't find it so fucking hot to see my cum slide out of her. I'd marked her in a primal way.

She was mine. I'd never wanted a woman the way I wanted her.

"Problem?" I asked with a smirk, knowing it would annoy her.

"Asshole," she muttered and reached for a tissue from a box on a nearby table.

After cleaning herself, she straightened her dress and took a deep, steadying breath.

Turning to face me, she lifted her dark gaze to mine, the annoyance gone and replaced by complete vulnerability.

"Can you handle being with someone who has a reputation, someone not perfect, someone with opinions?"

I moved in her direction, careful to move slowly, as if she would run at any moment.

When I stood before her, I placed a finger under her chin and brought her face up to meet my eyes. "I've acquired a taste for a goddess known for holding blades to throats and calling me an asshole."

She swallowed as if a lump had formed in her throat.

"Didn't you say you wanted someone who knew all your secrets? I know everything."

"I told you I want someone who I can share my secrets with and accepts me."

"Have I done anything to change you?" I rubbed a thumb over her lower lip. "No matter what you believe, some ordinary chump can't give you what you want. Besides, they'll never have the power to protect you."

"But with you, it means giving up all of this and the life I've built. It means going back to the cage."

"It's no more a cage than the one you're in here. There is no escaping the guards or twenty-four-seven eyes. Especially not with this side job of yours. Then there is the fact you're a Mykos for the rest of your life. That itself has a collar you will never escape. No matter where you go, someone could use you against them."

"And what about you? I would become a liability that people could use against you."

"I'm going to make sure no one can get to you, so that is a nonissue."

"Simon." Her hand came up to rest on my wrist. "Give me a real reason this is worth it."

She wanted the words. How the fuck was I going to say something I couldn't verbalize even if I tried?

Just as I opened my mouth to respond, a knock sounded on the door, leaving the heavy weight of my missing words between us.

I stared down at her, then shifted my attention to the door as another knock came and Stevie called from the other side, "Guys, the next set is about to start. We need Nyx on the floor."

"We'll continue this conversation at the end of the night." I stepped away from her and moved to where I'd thrown my jacket when we'd entered the room.

Reaching into the inside pocket of the suit, I pulled out a black pouch and returned to her. "Here, I have something for you."

Before she could move, I slipped a platinum necklace with a large teardrop diamond pendant around her neck.

Lifting the necklace, she examined it.

The slight pursing of her lips told me she'd discovered the secret inside the handcrafted pendant hanging from the chain.

"Don't you like it? Most women like gifts from their fiancé."

"You're not as slick as you think you are." She lifted a brow. "A tracker. Really?"

"Yes." I held her onyx gaze. "With the shit going on with Albert and Hal, I will do what's necessary to make sure you're safe."

"Meaning, you discovered people you thought were allies are actually not?"

"You seem to know more about my business than you should."

"I know about a lot of things."

"Then you understand my concern with your safety."

"What happened earlier had nothing to do with my safety."

"No, it revolved around making it clear to you and anyone else who looks in your direction that you belong to me."

"Possessive men are a turnoff."

I felt the tension and the emotional weight of our conversation from moments earlier lift. "Says the liar whose pussy is soaked in my cum."

"You're incorrigible." She shook her head.

I shrugged, pulling her toward me for a quick kiss before moving to the door and letting her pass.

As she made her way halfway down the hall, I called, "Goddess?"

"Yes." She glanced over her shoulder, and I felt as if my heart stopped.

I fucking loved this woman, and she hadn't a clue.

"You wanted a reason."

She nodded.

"I'll give you one after you close shop, then you decide. The ball is completely in your court."

"Really?"

"Yes."

Her lips trembled for a split second, then she nodded, turning to go into the main parlor of the penthouse.

———

TWO HOURS AFTER LEAVING NYX TO FINISH HER GAMING NIGHT, I arrived at a series of warehouses in a suburb near Las Vegas. I knew two things about the meeting that would occur in the next few minutes.

First, it was an epic waste of time, but necessary to keep Santos on a leash. Second, Santos wasn't aware that at this very moment, a group of my men was clearing out his shipping warehouse where Albert had stored my missing cargo.

I may have failed to become the exact image of Gio Drakos, but I had learned his ability to wait people out and watch them hang themselves. Once my freight sat safely in storage, I'd let my lieutenants handle the takeover of Santos's territory.

Motherfucker had no idea he'd messed with the wrong Drakos.

"This area is too quiet," Kasen observed as the car pulled to a stop and our men got into position.

"My thoughts exactly. Do you get the feeling this is some type of setup? No, I'm positive it's a setup."

"Albert has to know this is Draco's territory. Any move against you is like declaring war on him too."

My thoughts went to Nyx.

"We already know neither Albert nor Hal understand the order of things. Make sure everything is fine at the penthouse." I grabbed my revolver, tucking it into the waistband of my pants.

The hell if I'd take any chances.

"She's going to hand you your balls. Her team can handle anything."

"Just do it. Something about this doesn't feel right. Let me send a message to Sota. I'd rather err on the side of caution and have backup than end up dead on Draco's turf."

After sending my text to Sota, I stepped out of my car and made my way to the metal doors where Santos had indicated we'd meet.

I clenched my jaw, seeing nothing but a chair in the center of an empty space.

"There's an envelope on the seat," Kasen noticed and went to get it.

Opening it, he pulled out the contents and lifted an angry gaze to mine.

"We need to get back to Vegas now." He stalked toward me. "Keep it together."

I grabbed the stack of papers from him and looked down as a rage like nothing I'd felt filled my body. "I'm going to kill him. I'm going to kill every last one of them."

There were images of Nyx and me from our night on the balcony of her penthouse, every intimate detail of what had happened.

I clenched my jaw as I saw another image from tonight, through the living room windows of the suite where Nyx was right now. Her leaning back as I kissed her.

Whoever took those shots had a long-range camera, telling me someone had tipped them off about our location. And no one should have known about the game outside of the people Nyx had invited and our security teams.

I scanned the note attached. It might as well have sealed my uncle and his fucking son's death certificates.

DID THE DARKNESS FIND HIS NIGHT? IS SHE YOUR WEAKNESS? OR IS she a prize for all that comes with her? Remember, there is always another Drakos around to replace you if you can't make it to the altar.
    -Albert

I WAS DONE WITH THIS SHIT. NO MORE WAITING. NO MORE planning. He wanted a war, he'd get his fucking war. But first, I'd make goddamned sure no one touched my woman.

"Did you get in touch with anyone?" I moved toward the exit to the warehouse.

Kasen shook his head. "Something is off. No one can get in touch with anyone at the penthouse. Our men should have reported in within seconds, and it's radio science."

I gripped the back of my neck, and I'd barely made it over the threshold of the doorway when I heard, "Hello, nephew."

Kasen and a few of my other lieutenants threw their bodies over mine, blocking me from taking the bullet shot in my direction.

In the next second, chaos ensued, my men going into action as I rolled to the side, pulled out my gun, and prepared to end this bullshit once and for all.

The past no longer mattered, or avenging my parents and Gio. It was about my present and future.

Nyx.

21

NYX

I SIGHED AS THE LAST OF THE CLEANING CREW EXITED THE SUITE A little after two in the morning. Tonight's game seemed to have taken more out of me than usual. Maybe it was the emotions churning inside me from the intensity of my conversation with Simon.

Fuck. The last thing I ever expected out of my life was that I'd end up wanting to spend it as the other half of a syndicate head.

He wasn't supposed to matter. The thought of him not being in my life shouldn't make me want to cry. He'd fucking blackmailed me into this shit.

Lifting my tumbler to my lips, I swallowed down a healthy gulp of whiskey. The smooth, potent spirit heated my insides and gave me a small sense of calmness.

Stevie came toward me and nodded in an indication that she and her team had secured our take for tonight's event.

"Want to watch a movie like old times until he gets here?" I asked, offering Stevie a serving of the amber goodness.

"We won't even get through the opening credits. Let's just have a drink or two."

"How the fuck did I get here?" I asked and then dropped my head into my hand.

"You have a thing for assholes. It's your kink."

I glared at her and then shook my head. "Only one asshole. I don't understand when it changed."

"You're kidding, right?"

"What?"

"It happened that first day when he caught you on your knees in the garden. He had you under his thrall with those fucking green eyes of his with one look. Hell, I can't stand him most of the time, and even I'm not immune to them."

"If I remember correctly, you and Akari were the ones who wanted him to become my booty call." I ran a hand over my face. "What am I going to do?"

"Can you see yourself walking away?"

The thought of it left a painful ache deep in my heart. But then again, the idea of going back to New York wasn't something I ever planned.

"I'd have to deal with the bullshit again."

"You deal with it just fine here. The only difference there is that they aren't tourists and don't think you're an employee of the hotel."

"You up for a move to New York?"

Stevie cocked her head to the side and studied me. "I guess you made the decision?"

"Looks that way."

"Then all you have to do is tell him. But I suggest you make him work for it a little longer. Things come to him too easily."

I shook my head. "You're as incorrigible as he is."

She shrugged.

At that moment, a ring sounded on the elevator, making both Stevie and me jump up. No one should be able to access it.

We had it on lockdown. Even Simon would have to call up to get inside.

That's when I felt the tip of a gun pressed to the back of my head, and the sounds of some type of fight behind me.

"Don't move, Nyx," Justin, one of Simon's men, ordered, grabbing me by my upper arm. "Tell your girl to stop struggling or she'll end up like the rest of her people."

I swallowed, trying to push away the fear prickling down my spine, and glanced at Stevie, who was in a headlock and pinned to the ground.

"Stevie," I whispered. "Please. Remember the number-one rule you told me."

Hearing the plea in my voice, she followed my request.

The rule she taught me was to do everything to stay alive, including let my assailant believe I'd yielded.

I had no doubt she'd keep looking for opportunities to get out of this situation. I had to keep this guy talking, keep them distracted. That was the only way to figure this out.

Right before Simon had left for his meeting, he'd handed me one of my blades and ordered me to strap it to my thigh. I'd thought he'd gone a little overboard with the around-the-clock double security team, the necklace, and the blade.

Now, I owed him the blowjob of his life.

If this was happening here, what could have happened at the meeting?

I closed my eyes for a brief second and prayed Simon stayed safe.

"Who ordered this?" I asked, trying to keep Justin's attention on me.

A smug grin touched his mouth. "Mr. Drakos."

Bullshit.

"Liar. Simon wouldn't do this."

"Wrong Drakos."

That was when from the corner of my eye, I noticed Tony sprawled on the ground, blood dripping from the side of his head.

All my intentions of staying poised vanished as my stomach clenched, and without realizing it, I elbowed him in the ribs. "You bastard."

"Calm the fuck down." He pinned my arms behind my back. "He's not dead. We don't have time to clean the mess."

Thank God for small favors.

"I don't understand why you'd do this. You're one of Simon's men."

"Wrong. I'm Gio's. I knew from the beginning Kyros's son was soft like him. You are a liability, just like his mother was."

"How the fuck am I a liability?"

"You've changed his priorities. We've watched it happen. Now we'll use it to shift the power to the rightful Drakos. Albert understands the way of things, as does Hal."

"The rightful Drakos is in power," I gritted out. "Taking me won't change it. My brothers will destroy you."

"Keep thinking that. They've signed on as allies to Albert."

"Not a chance." I shook my head.

I knew all of it was bullshit. Papa hated Albert for his treatment of my mother during their youth. Papa had a way of letting people believe he'd support them without outright giving a formal commitment, which never bound him to do anything.

Ignoring my words, he gestured with his chin to another man. "Open the cab. Let them in."

A second later, the doors opened, and Hal stepped out with a group of men I recognized from the engagement party. All of them belonging to families that were supposed to be allies of my father and brothers.

Oh God, this couldn't be happening.

Hal's attention zoomed in on me, and he strode in my direction. My assessment of him from that night in the botanical gardens was beyond accurate. He couldn't hold a candle to Simon in the way he carried himself.

Hal tried too hard to emulate his older cousin and failed—in style, swagger, everything.

Yeah, my opinion was skewed in favor of Simon, but it made it no less the truth.

Damn, I sounded like a lovesick puppy, even in my head.

"Hello, princess. Or should I call you goddess, as Simon prefers?"

"Nyx will do." I glared at him. "What do you want?"

"I have a proposition." He threw a coin on the table behind me. "Something I encourage you to consider in exchange for keeping your secret from going public. Have a seat."

Not waiting to see if I'd comply, Justin forced me down into my seat and then stepped back.

"Go see if you can find the footage for tonight's game and the lockbox."

I smirked. They'd never find it. We hid it in a different location after every event, and the only people who knew the exact spot to search were Stevie and me.

"You don't scare me, Hal."

"It's not my intention to scare you. You should have met with me that day instead of standing me up. It would have saved us this trouble."

"You mean holding me against my will in a hotel room?"

"Hotel suites are your specialty. Although, you do seem to enjoy penthouse balconies for some of your more engaging activities. You and my cousin gave my men quite the show. Live-action porn at its best."

My face heated, remembering how Simon and I were so lost in primal need that after the initial worry, I hadn't given any more thought to the idea of anyone watching us.

"Just so you know, that shit won't fly with me. I don't fuck in public."

I frowned, cocking my head a little, studying his face. He gave me a deadpan stare as if I was stupid for not understanding his meaning.

He couldn't be serious.

Hell, no.

"You actually think I'm going to jump from one Drakos to another? Simon isn't replaceable."

"Then your family forfeits the trust. Or we can just make it happen now, by divulging your illegal business dealings."

"A poker chip and one random picture don't prove anything. Kids do all kinds of things when they are eighteen."

Annoyance flashed on his face, and he moved in my direction, stopping when he was right upon me.

"What about your friend, David Stafenavos? I'm sure he can dig up information on your current endeavors."

"Once again, it is the word of a disgruntled former friend, who I refuse to have any form of communication with. You. Have. No. Proof. Your plan has a few holes."

He grabbed hold of my hair, jerking me out of the chair, and sending a shockwave of pain through my scalp. "This hellion act won't work with me. I'm not soft like Simon."

"That is the last thing anyone would say about him." I dug my nails into Hal's arm, drawing blood, and then bit out, "You're dead when he gets here."

Correction. He was dead when I fucking got my hand on my blade. I planned to gut the motherfucker into tiny little pieces.

He shook off my hand, forcing me facedown onto the high sideboard table. "It's his death you need to worry about. There is a high chance his meeting hasn't gone as planned. Then you'll have no choice but to honor the contract with me."

All the blood drained from my face. No, Simon was too smart to walk into a trap.

"Keep dreaming. Your father tried to kill him before. I doubt you'll do any better a job than he did."

His hold in my hair tightened as he leaned down and seethed through gritted teeth, "Outside of your looks, I can't understand what Simon sees in you."

Just as I was about to respond, someone came out of the primary bedroom and announced, "The lockbox isn't here. She must have given it to her friend Akari."

"Then send someone to retrieve it," Hal ordered.

Justin hesitated as a frown marred his face. "She's essentially Draco Jackson's granddaughter."

"I don't give a fuck who she is."

Hal couldn't be so stupid. He had to know Draco would take it personally if anyone thought to go near Akari. He had people watching her day and night.

"It could start a war."

"We're already at war. What is one more?"

What a dumbass.

When Hal pulled me back, eyes blazing and fury on his face, I realized I'd spoken my thought out loud.

"This dumbass isn't the one who left his woman unprotected."

That was when I caught Stevie's nod, telling me it was time to stop my verbal game of bratty socialite and bring out my inner Harley.

I had no clue what Stevie had accomplished while I kept this idiot occupied, but I understood my part in this whole charade.

Though, I'd never actually done it on a human.

Livestock, yes. Humans, no.

Taking a deep breath, I set one hand on my thigh as I clutched at the one Hal maintained on my scalp, letting him believe he had control of me.

As he took a step back, I pretended to stumble, grabbed the hilt of the blade resting comfortably in the sheath strapped to my inner thigh, and then, a second later, I sliced straight through Hal's side.

He flinched, and then his body jerked backward, taking me with him. We both landed on the ground, in a hard fall of limbs.

A wave of dizziness hit me as his weight knocked the wind out of me, followed by a rush of nausea. Breathing through the pain, I struggled to free myself from Hal's bleeding form.

"Get off me, you bastard." I shoved at him, his blood covering my hand, making it hard to move him.

He clutched at his ribs as he tried to lock an arm around my waist. I managed to kick him in the stomach and crouched before he could grab hold of my midsection.

I crawled where I last remembered seeing Stevie. I heard the echo of gunshots booming in my ear. Ducking down, I hid against the back of a sofa and noticed the open service elevator in the far corner of the penthouse kitchen.

It wasn't open earlier. In fact, it was hidden behind a moving wall.

That was when I saw him.

His gun was drawn, dried blood on the corner of his temple, clothes torn, his face a play of fury, and his body set in a stance that screamed he'd kill anyone who got in his way.

He shouted orders right and left as people moved in to take over the penthouse.

"S-Simon," I whispered, feeling both a sense of relief and fear.

I'd never seen him like this.

Holy fuck. Was this hot?

His green gaze connected with mine a second before he lifted his revolver in my direction. Closing my eyes, I waited for the bullet to pierce its intended target and the distinct thud of the body hitting the floor to reach my ears before I opened my lids.

Simon knelt before me, worry haunting his eyes.

"Goddess, let me take this." He touched my hand.

I glanced down, not realizing I still held the carved hilt of the blade. All the adrenaline of the situation had probably pushed me to keep my defenses up.

This was so damn gross. I had Hal guts on me.

"My brothers are going to give me such a hard time about this, especially Tyler." I flexed my blood-soaked fingers and looked up at Simon, sighing. "I'm supposed to make them bleed out, but not all over me. Those are the rules."

"Your brothers aren't normal by any standards. Most sisters don't get lessons in gutting people."

I shrugged. "They're all I know."

With his thumb and index finger, Simon took the knife from me, and on cue, one of his men stepped up next to him with a cloth, wrapped it tight, and bagged it.

"I'll have it cleaned and returned, sir."

Simon inclined his head without taking his attention from me.

"Now we need to get you checked out." He brushed the hair back from the side of my face, more than likely seeing the bruise forming there from when Hal had pushed my head down onto the table.

He shifted his attention over to where Hal lay on the ground and clenched his jaw. "I left you unprotected. It won't happen again."

"It wasn't your fault."

"The hell it wasn't. This was a setup, and I walked into it." Simon dropped his forehead to mine. "They used Santos to distract me with a meeting and then ambushed me so this fucker could get to you."

"Simon, you came. That's what matters."

He touched my necklace. "What good did it do?"

"I'm fine." I covered his fingers on the pendant with mine. "I just need to clean up."

Before I could say anything else, he scooped me into his arms and carried me to the primary bedroom of the suite.

"We can't leave this place until they get everything swept and serviced," Simon stated. "Then I plan to take care of the rest of them."

I felt the unleashed wrath bubbling in him.

"I know how things work. Don't forget whose daughter I am."

He moved into the giant bathroom and set me on the counter.

His gaze met mine. "Then you also understand what your father would do if your mother were in the place you were in tonight."

A shiver ran down my spine.

Stepping away from me, Simon turned on the shower and then returned with a washcloth, setting it on the counter near me.

Then he unzipped my dress, pulling it over my head and tossing it to the floor. Next went my underwear. When I was naked, he reached for a cloth towel, soaked it with water from the sink, and then began to wash the blood from my skin.

The way he stroked over my body, so softly, so delicately,

made me believe he thought I'd break if he touched me too hard.

He tugged my engagement ring off, rinsed it, and then brought it to the light.

"Only you will ever wear this. It means you're mine, Goddess." He slid it back on my finger. "I will make sure no one even thinks of touching you again."

I grabbed hold of his wrist, forcing him to look at me. "I'm fine."

"You don't get it, Nyx. I could have lost you."

"I'm here. I know how to use my blades. He was bleeding out even before you got to me."

"And what would have happened afterward? I won't ever risk it again."

"You can't be with me all the time. I live in a different city. Besides, this was temporary."

"Things changed. You can't deny it."

The intensity of his gaze had my lips trembling.

"Even if you do, I'm keeping you, whether you want it or not." He cupped my cheek and then rubbed his thumb over my lower lip. "Haven't you figured it out? I'm about to wage a war because someone touched you. Hell, I'd fucking burn this world down."

A tear slipped down my cheek, and without another thought, I fisted his shirt and tugged him toward me, sealing our mouths together.

His arms came around me, molding my body to his hard, hot, aroused one. We ate at each other's mouths, devouring as if we couldn't quench this need. Our tongues sliding, molding, tasting, consuming.

I ground my pussy against his thick cock, needing the friction to ease the ache deep inside my core.

I burned for him. It tore at me how much I needed him. This man who I wanted to hate so desperately when we met and now couldn't imagine being without.

"Simon," I whimpered, clenching at his hair. "I need more, please."

He lifted me by my thighs, folding my legs around his hips, and stepped inside the steaming shower.

"You're fully clothed," I exclaimed.

He slid me to the floor and then toed his shoes off and said, "Then undress me."

"So bossy." I went to work on the buttons of his soaked shirt, pushing it from his shoulders.

"If you haven't figured it out by now, I've been doing something wrong for months."

By the time he was naked, I was panting and desperate for him to fuck me.

"Do you want gentle or hard?"

"I get a choice?"

"You're hurt." He brushed the side of my face, anger flaring in his eyes again.

Twining my arms around his neck, I lifted onto tiptoes. "I want us. Raw, dirty, and depraved. Just like you promised that first night together."

He gripped my waist, a war of emotions playing over his face. "I didn't have a chance with you, did I?"

"You surprised the fuck out of me too." I brushed my mouth against his. "Though you'll always be the asshole who blackmailed me."

His lips curved up. "I am who I am. Now, turn around and brace your arms on the wall."

Following his directions, I barely had a chance to steady myself before he grabbed hold of my hip, kicked my legs apart, positioned himself, and thrust in.

"Oh God. Simon," I cried out, the pleasure-pain of his invasion blurring my vision and firing every nerve in my body to life.

"You asked for it." He wrapped his forearm across my chest and cupped my throat.

I stared at his beautiful face, water dripping from the curls fallen onto his forehead.

My palms flexed on the wall. "I did. Now do it more. I need you to fuck me like you mean it. Don't be gentle."

"Is this what you want?" He pulled out and thrust back in so hard that he had me coming onto my tiptoes.

"Yes," I whimpered, the heady mix of sensations of his thick cock inside me and possessive grip on my neck filling my mind with a euphoria I never seemed to stop craving. "That's...that's exactly what I want."

"This is why you're mine." With those words, he set a brutal, wickedly delicious pace. One that gave me no leverage, one that gave him all the control, one that only allowed me to take.

My pussy quickened, flexing, clamping, and flooding as my orgasm approached. My clit throbbed, needing just the slightest stroke, and I would detonate.

I shifted my hand on the wall, ready to give my body the relief it begged for. But some part of me resisted, knowing this man's touch was what I craved.

"Simon, please. I fucking need to come."

His fingers slid down my stomach to my clit. The moment he grazed the sensitive bundle of nerves, his teeth clamped down on my shoulder.

"Yes," I cried out as all the breath left my body, and my mind clouded with wave after wave of ecstasy.

My pussy clamped down on his pistoning cock. His pace never wavered, no matter how hard my pussy walls flexed and contracted.

"It's too much." The orgasm shook my entire body, leaving me limp and unable to stand.

"We're not done yet."

"You can't be serious."

"Very serious."

Simon strummed my clit, bringing me to the cusp of another release and then pinching the bundle of nerves, skyrocketing me into another mind-blowing cascade of pleasure, but this time, he shattered with me.

22

SIMON

"WHAT IS THIS ABOUT, MYKOS?" I GLARED AT TYLER AS HE LAZILY entered the hotel suite he'd summoned me to an hour earlier.

The fucker made it sound as if we were on the verge of some major crisis, but from the intel Kasen had given me, they had nothing brewing at the moment.

On the other hand, I was neck-deep in clearing the last of Albert and Hal's supports within my house and those who claimed to be my allies. Eliminating Albert and Hal had made it harder to identify everyone, but it would happen.

"We'll get to it. Why don't you get comfortable? We have some important matters to discuss."

"Move it along. I have other things on my agenda today besides wasting time with you."

Nyx was scheduled to arrive anytime this morning, and my

plans involved us leaving for a trip on one of my ships off the coast of Maine.

"Yes, I heard about your upcoming weekend sea voyage."

His tone had me pausing, as did the annoyance on the faces of the other Mykos brothers.

Tyler moved toward me, opened a folder, and then positioned a set of photos in front of me. Each of the pictures showed Nyx and me at various places in Vegas. Thank God none of them were of us from that damn balcony.

Fuck.

I glanced around and realized Phillip Mykos was absent from the meeting. The fact he wasn't present made it clear his sons wanted this conversation kept from him.

Tyler tapped the picture with Nyx curled against me as we sat on the terrace of her Las Vegas penthouse. I held her tight and watched her sleep.

It was the night following the aftermath of the bullshit with Hal a month earlier.

She looked so fragile in my arms. She trusted me to protect her, and I'd nearly failed.

I *had* fucking failed. If I'd paid more attention, then she wouldn't have had to filet the fucker.

I scanned a series of other pictures. Ones where we danced at nightclubs, explored parts of Vegas, and others of us in her greenhouse and cottage.

They damn well knew I was there the whole fucking time.

Dickheads.

There was one thing all of the images proved to anyone who saw them. Nyx was my woman, my weakness. The one way to get to me.

"What are you going to do about it?"

"She's my fiancée. What is there to do about it? I can spend time with her, and in any manner as I deem necessary."

"If that's how you want to play it, we can play it your way." Tyler leaned back in his chair. "Do you actually think I don't know what my sister does in Vegas? She's had her security wrapped around her finger since she was sixteen. I couldn't trust them to report everything to me. I have my own people mixed in with hers.

"I love my sister and have complete confidence in her abilities and intelligence, but we both know she doesn't have the ruthlessness necessary to survive the things she likes to dangle her feet into. I know about her clubs, her side businesses, her friendships, and I know about your deal. You son of a bitch. I ought to kill you for doing that to her."

I gave no outward reaction to his words, only asked, "And you let it play out?"

"Nyx isn't a little girl. She's a grown woman. If she got in too far with you, I'd have stepped in."

"Is that why you're here? You think she's in too deep."

"You both are." A smirk touched his lips, but the anger in his eyes conveyed how much he wanted to wipe the floor with me. "Didn't go according to plan, did it, Drakos? It wasn't supposed to get personal. She wasn't supposed to matter."

"Is there a point to this?"

His face grew serious. "If you love her, you let her go. She isn't cut out for this life. I told you this from the fucking start. All she ever wanted was her freedom. I won't let you trap her."

"What makes you think she can't handle it?"

"She can handle anything, but it isn't what she wants. Why

do you think I sent her to Vegas? She's too smart to be someone's arm candy."

"The last thing I would ever expect of her is to hold that position."

"She needs someone without our baggage, and you know it. Do you think your uncle and cousin are the last of the bastards who will use her to get to you? You have a slew of enemies who would love to find a way to break you. My sister won't become collateral damage for a man like you."

"What makes you think I have any feelings for her?"

"Those pictures show a man who'd burn the world down for her," Evan observed. "From what I hear, you cleaned house of anyone rumored to have any involvement in the incident with Nyx."

No one outside of my men was supposed to know the truth behind my war with my uncle. Now it looked as if Stevie and Tony had a set of eyes in their organizational structure sending information to the Mykos brothers.

"I don't tolerate traitors."

"Bullshit. You don't just throw away a decade of planning to take down your biggest enemy for anyone." Tyler learned back in his chair. "How many are dead for targeting her? How many are out in the wind for thinking to use her against you? How many of your people watch out for her safety in addition to her own?"

"Anyone would take care of their fiancée in a similar fashion."

"Keep telling yourself that."

"Spell it out for me, Mykos. What is it that you want me to do?"

"Break it off."

"By doing that, are you willing to forego such a large sum?"

"For my sister's happiness, absolutely. But we know you aren't going to actually end the engagement. You will end your personal relationship and just hold to the formal aspects."

"She won't like that you are interfering."

"You aren't going to tell her. This is between us. She won't ever learn that I know anything about her activities in Vegas."

"Why wouldn't I disclose this?"

"Because I will still honor the port transfer. It technically belonged to your family generations ago, anyway."

"Your sister's happiness is worth that much to you?"

"The question is, what is it worth to you?"

Everything.

I held his cold gaze with one of my own, not saying anything.

Fucker knew he had me by the balls.

"You're lucky I didn't kill you for the terms of your arrangement in the first place. But seeing as it brought you to your knees, I can live with it." Tyler rose from his chair. "As I said, if you love her, then you let her go. Give her the freedom she craves so damn much."

"What makes you think she won't pick me?"

"It's not a matter of picking you or not. You're not going to give her an option. Wasn't that how it all started? Blackmailing her into your arrangement?"

"I have no incentive for letting her go."

"How about this? The second you break it off with her, I will hand over the port. I won't make you wait out the rest of the term for the contract."

"You're trying to bribe me?"

"This is no different than before. But wait"—he paused, a calculating smirk touching his lips—"it is. You're in love with her. You have to weigh what's worth more to you. My sister or something to expand your empire."

He knew damn well there was no competition.

"I can make her happy."

"Maybe. But you don't deserve her. No one from our world does. With you, she will stay a target. That's not the life I want for her."

"That's not your choice to make."

"But it's yours." Tyler leaned forward. "Stop being a selfish prick for one second and think about her. What did she say she wanted from the moment she met you? Can you honestly give her that one thing?"

Freedom.

"You want me to hurt her."

"It's better for her to heal from a broken heart than live a life she doesn't want. Sooner or later, she'll find someone who can give her a normal life."

"Would anyone know normal when they grew up the way we have?"

"I'd rather her try to find out than risk another fucker using her life to get to you."

I remained quiet, knowing he was right. I couldn't bear the idea of anything happening to her. Though the day she found someone else would actually kill the heart I never thought existed.

After a few moments, I nodded.

"As always, it's a pleasure doing business with you."

"This isn't business. She's not business."

"Finally, you understand how we feel." He studied me. "There is this saying my mother uses to describe her relationship with my father."

I waited for him to continue.

"If you love someone, set them free. If they come back, they're yours."

Nyx had mentioned her parents had separated in their youth and then gotten back together, but never the details.

"Let her go, and if you end up together, I won't stand in the way. But give her a chance at the life she's always wanted."

"Is that what your father did?"

Tyler shook his head. "It was my mother. It took her nearly marrying another man for my father to get his head on straight. Those are his words, not hers."

The Mykoses were definitely unlike any other family.

"I'll take care of it." I stood, feeling as if my world was crashing around me, and walked out of the hotel suite.

TWENTY MINUTES LATER, I ENTERED THE LOUNGE ADJACENT TO my home office. Nyx sat cross-legged on the floor, leaning against a coffee table while shuffling a deck of cards and reading something on the computer in front of her.

She lifted her gaze from the screen and smiled. "Hey, ready for me to kick your ass at some poker before we start our weekend voyage?"

Had anyone's eyes ever lit up with happiness when I walked into a room? Worry and fear, but only ever joy with her.

Now, I was about to fuck it all to hell.

The one time in my life I would do the right thing, I was going to destroy the only thing that meant anything to me.

"What's wrong?" She set the cards on the table and came toward me.

"We need to talk."

She studied me, a crease of worry settling between her brows. "That sounds ominous."

"Your brother offered me the Cyprus port free and clear."

Confusion flashed on her face. "Okay. Why is that a bad thing? That was the long-term plan, anyway."

I moved to the windows in the back of the room to put distance between us and then faced her.

"It means your brother fulfilled his portion of our agreement early. Now all that's left is to play out the terms of the engagement contract."

"Meaning?"

"Meaning, this. You and me." I gestured between us while swallowing down the rancid lump forming in my throat. "It's over. You're free."

"W-what?" She braced her hand on the back of the fabric-covered chair.

"You heard me."

"So, all of this was about the port?"

"Yes."

"Bullshit." She clenched her jaw. "What was all that about keeping me whether I wanted to stay or not? What was all that about burning down the world for me?"

Shit.

"You shouldn't read too much into it. A man will say anything when he's balls-deep in a woman's cunt."

"And the war with your uncle and his allies. You changed everything because they came after me."

"Don't romanticize events. It was a strategic change of plans."

She flinched. "Again. Bullshit. That's not what happened, and you know it. Explain to me what you meant when you stated only I would ever wear this ring."

She lifted her left hand.

I turned toward the window, gripped the back of my neck, and prepared to become the bastard my grandfather had raised me to be.

Fuck, I hated myself at this moment.

Shifting to look in her direction, I kept my face emotionless as I said, "You couldn't possibly believe I'd change my mind about marrying you. You knew who I picked from the beginning. You aren't her. This was all about sex. Fucking to pass the time."

The starkness in her onyx eyes told me I'd landed a direct blow, though the expressionless mask she wore would have made anyone else believe otherwise. Anyone who hadn't seen every facet of her, from utter joy to raging anger. Now, I could add complete devastation to the list.

"So, it's still Camilla, even after her father's involvement with your uncle. After all the shit she pulled with us."

"Yes. She knows her place in my world, what is expected of her."

She flinched as if I'd hit her, and it took everything in me not to reach for her, to tell her I was a fucking liar.

"And I guess I know mine now too." She held my gaze. "I don't have one."

"Exactly. You're free. Isn't that what you wanted? Well, now you have it. Your club is safe. My lips are sealed. Make a life for yourself in Vegas."

"If that's how you want to play it. Fine." She pulled the ring from her finger and set it on a side table with the computer. "This is yours. Give me something meaningless to wear for show."

"You'll soon realize this is best for both of us."

"Keep telling yourself that if it makes you feel better. You won't have to see me any more than necessary." A tear slid down her cheek. "But I know the truth."

"What's that?"

"I became exactly what your grandfather warned you against, and now you're running scared."

She moved to the door, turning the handle. Just as she opened the door to step through, she paused and glanced at me.

"I was going to leave Vegas for you. That's how much I love you. Asshole that you are, and all. Too bad I was so wrong about you."

With those words, Nyx shut the door and took the last decent part of my soul with her.

I had to remind myself this was the right thing to do.

She deserved better than me. A life without people using her to get to me. A life without her having to sacrifice her choices.

She could escape this world.

Bracing my hands on the back of a nearby sofa and dropping my head, I clenched my eyes tight.

"Fuck."

Not even ten minutes later, my phone rang, and without thinking, I pulled it out of my pocket and answered, "Drakos."

"The port is yours. The paperwork will arrive at your office in the morning."

"How the fuck do you know anything happened?"

Could she have had time to reach her brothers?

"Nyx called saying she is coming into town and wants to practice with her blades. That's my sign she's upset and needs to let off steam."

"I didn't do it for the port."

"I know. As I told you in our meeting, if she comes back to you, then she's yours."

"There is no chance of that ever happening. I made sure of it."

The pain I'd caused her would remain etched in my heart for the rest of my life. Mykos was right—she deserved a life away from me, away from the shit of our world. Now she'd get her chance.

"She really does mean that much to you, doesn't she?"

"It's done. That's all you need to know."

"You're a better man than I expected."

"None of us are good men. We do what's most advantageous for the long game."

"Long game, is it?"

"Yes."

"I see." He remained quiet for a second and then said, "Well, consider the Mykoses among your allies to back you in future endeavors. All past grievances are null and void."

Tyler hung up.

I sat down on a high-back chair, trying to process what had just transpired.

I'd finally done what generations of Drakoses and Mykoses could never accomplish. I had ended a century-old rivalry, one that had cost millions of dollars and countless lives. And all I'd had to do was destroy the best thing that had ever happened to me.

23

NYX

SIX WEEKS TO THE DAY SINCE LEAVING SIMON'S HOUSE, I LEANED against the railing of my apartment balcony and enjoyed the view of the Vegas night sky.

Lifting my face into the warm summer breeze, I sighed. This was my first night off in weeks, and the only things on my agenda included cocktails and maybe a movie or two.

Alone.

The last thing I wanted was anyone around.

It seemed as if everyone and their dog thought I was going to fall apart at any moment. Why couldn't they understand people handled pain differently?

I channeled all my hurt and rage into work. It kept me from thinking too much and gave me an outlet.

It was when I wasn't busy that thoughts crept in and the

pain started choking me, therefore work solved all of my issues. And made me wealthier in the process.

Since coming back from New York, I'd run ten Silent Night Club events throughout Vegas, drawing in some of the biggest whales from around the world.

I realized I was pushing my luck during last night's event when I'd learned the FBI had raided an underground poker ring in another part of town. Therefore, I'd made the call to close shop for at least two months.

Now, I had to find something else to occupy my time.

Dropping my head to the railing, I groaned.

"How did I guess I'd find you here," I heard Akari say from behind me. "You're coming with me."

I glared over my shoulder at Stevie. "What's the point of you being my security if you let people in?"

"She has a key. I assumed that she was an exception."

I shifted my attention to Akari. "I'm not going anywhere, so you can turn around."

Acting as if I hadn't said anything to her, Akari moved in my direction. She held a mug in her hand, and I had a sneaky suspicion it contained one of her spiked teas I loved so much.

Bitch was trying to bribe me.

At least if she was going to disturb my night in, she brought something.

"The destination I have in mind has some of the best nightlife in the world."

"Vegas has some of the best nightlife in the world. I'm good here."

"Here. Drink this." Akari handed me the mug. "It will help

lighten your mood. And then I'll show you something that I'm positive will convince you to jump on the jet with me."

Taking the cup from her, I inhaled the rich aroma of tea and whiskey and then took a deep gulp.

"Okay, spill what you want to tell me and then go away. Nothing is going to get me to leave this apartment. I want to veg."

"Originally, I'd planned to Nyx-nap you and whisk you away to Bora Bora, but some recent information concerning you has made me change our destination."

I cocked my head to the side and then studied her. "You've got my curiosity piqued."

"He lied to you."

"Who?"

"Your asshole."

I swallowed. He wasn't mine. He'd all but destroyed my heart. No, he *had* destroyed it.

"He's not mine."

"Did you hear me? He lied."

"What are you talking about?"

"I went to see *Ojiisan* Draco, and I happened to overhear a conversation about Simon."

"What? Is he with some debutante?"

"No, that's just it. People don't see him unless it's for business. Want to know where he goes to think?" She air-quoted the last part.

I rolled my eyes. "Okay, I'll bite. Where?"

"Your greenhouse."

I swallowed. "What?"

"From what I heard, he drives out there at least twice a week, sits inside for hours, and then leaves."

My stomach clenched as a grain of hope settled.

"Are you sure the source you heard this information from is reliable? Some of Draco's grandsons are gossips and rarely have all the details right."

She sighed. "This actually came from Sota. It's his apology for revealing your club to Simon in the first place."

I knew it was him. Asshole.

With shaky hands, I took her phone, and immediately tears welled up in my eyes.

He'd lied to me.

I traced the picture of him at the beach with Sota and a few of the Jackson clan. He sat shirtless, and on his chest over his heart sat a tattoo with the word *goddess* in Greek.

"I guess this proves not everything is always as it seems. He isn't the typical guy from our world, after all."

"Aren't you the one who kept advocating for me to escape, to find my freedom?"

"Yeah, well, you fell in love with the booty call." The humor of her words never reached her eyes.

"What aren't you telling me?"

"I realized I was projecting my issues with my family onto you, and it wasn't fair. You fit pretty well. If he is what you want, confront him and see where it goes."

Stevie cocked a hip on the back of one of the sofas. "I agree. He's as miserable as you are. Go see him."

"What did he do to win you over so much?" I studied Stevie.

"He sacrificed what he wanted to give you what you wanted.

Your freedom. He put you first. That says a lot. That man loves you."

"He broke my heart," I murmured, remembering the devastation of the words he'd spoken to me.

"To give you the freedom you insisted you wanted." Stevie's voice grew hard. "It's all you've ever talked about. You didn't want to be trapped. You want to know who's trapped? He's the one trapped."

"How is he trapped?" I questioned.

"He can't ever leave his world, just like your brothers can't. Just like my brothers can't. He gave you the escape that you wanted." Akari set a hand on my leg. "Be honest. Is it really something you want or just the idea of it?"

I'd thought about it for weeks, and I'd made the decision a while ago. "I'd changed my mind even before everything imploded."

"For him?" Stevie probed.

I shook my head. "No, for me. The shit I do couldn't fly in the real world."

"Do you really think some normal guy with a nine-to-five could handle even half of your friends?" Akari laughed. "He'd piss himself the second Petre showed up at your door with his stories of enemies and drinking blood."

I stood, knowing what I had to do.

"Where are you going?" Stevie stood with me, giving me a curious once-over.

"To New York. I have to knock some sense into the asshole I plan to marry."

SIMON

I OPENED THE GATE CONNECTING THE GREENHOUSE AND GARDEN in the back of Nyx's cottage, wondering for the tenth time why the hell I'd driven here again. If any of the Mykos guards caught me, they'd probably believe I'd lost my mind.

For the last month, it was the only place I could get any semblance of peace from all the work piling up on my plate. I still had plenty of rot to clear from my household, but the removal of Albert and Hal from the family structure had solidified my seat as the head of Drakos Shipping. Now, all that was left was weeding out the true allies from the enemies.

Tyler had followed through with his agreement and transferred the port, and the transition had brought with it all the normal power bullshit with rivals in the area. Most of which Kasen handled since anything to do with the Mykoses reminded me of the one Mykos I couldn't have.

Though, it didn't mean I hadn't kept an eye on her. It seemed as if she'd thrown herself even deeper into her clubs and lost any sense of self-preservation, or maybe it was a dare for me to come for her.

I'd almost pulled the trigger and flown out there to tell her to rein in her activities. But I'd known it would have made things worse, and I refused to cause her any more pain.

The last pictures I'd gotten showed her sitting on her terrace staring out at a Vegas sunset.

God, I really was a fucking stalker, knowing everything that happened in her life.

Bracing my palm against the iron gates leading into the

maze section of the garden, I closed my eyes and saw in vivid detail the pain etched across Nyx's face as she'd told me she'd fallen in love with me.

I really was an asshole.

No. I'd done the right thing. It was the only way to give her the life she deserved. She would have given up her dream.

Cupping the back of my neck, I gazed up at the sky. I'd lived my whole life by the rules of one man, only to realize I'd failed him because I was more like the son he wanted to erase from existence.

However, I'd managed the one thing my father could never have done. I destroyed the only thing that ever meant anything to me.

Fuck, I needed to get out of here.

That's when I felt a presence behind me and froze. If it was Tyler, I'd punch him. The last thing I wanted to deal with was his cocky ass.

"Excuse me, this isn't your greenhouse. Why are you in it?"

I froze.

Nyx.

What the fuck was she doing here?

"Goddess, don't give me any shit."

"Why would I give you shit? Besides the fact this is a restricted area and you're trespassing."

I kept my gaze on the gardens, knowing if I looked in her direction, I'd want to reach for her, touch her.

"Nothing to say, Mr. Drakos?"

"I thought Akari was going to take you on a girls' trip to Bora Bora."

"How would you know what anyone in my world is doing?"

"I know."

"How?"

"I know everything about you."

"Why?"

I was quiet for a few seconds, then confessed, "To make sure you're safe."

"I see."

"What do you see?"

"That you're a fucking liar."

"What am I lying about?"

"Look me in the eyes and tell me it didn't become real."

"Does it matter?" I ran a frustrated hand through my hair. "I gave you what you want."

"What is it you think I want?"

"Your freedom."

"Am I really free? My heart doesn't feel that way. Besides, you were right. I can't leave this world being who I am and what I do."

"There is no more marriage contract. You're free," I repeated. "Now we just wait out the formal period."

"Do you love me, Simon?"

More than anything on Earth.

Instead of saying the words in my head, I said, "Don't ask me that."

"Why? Will it make you feel better if you keep telling yourself it was just sex?"

I clenched my fists at my sides, resisting the urge to turn and pull her to me. "You know it was more. I fucking told you things I never told anyone else."

"Then answer the question. Do you love me?"

"Isn't there a saying, if you love someone, set them free? I won't hold you to a life you don't want."

"Are you saying you love me? Well, I have a question for you."

I waited.

"Aren't you worth loving?"

"Goddess." I gripped the iron bars, dropping my head.

"You love me enough to let me go. Isn't my love for you enough to stay?"

"I won't trap you. You told me not to trap you."

"I grew up in this world. I'm pretty good at handling it. Not sure if you know this, but I'm so good at navigating things, society calls me the Mykos Hellion."

"And what about your life in Vegas? Are you ready to give that up?"

"You're worth giving all of that up." Her hand settled on my back. "You didn't finish it."

"Finish what?"

"The saying about loving someone and setting them free. You only quoted part of it."

Before I realized what I was doing, I reached around me, grabbed her wrist, and pulled her in front of me, pinning her back to the gate and her arms above her head.

"Goddess, don't." I stared at her beautiful flushed face. "Don't do it."

She smiled up at me. "Don't what?"

"Don't finish it."

"Why?" She lifted her chin.

"If you do, I won't let you go."

"I'm not asking you to. In fact, I want the very opposite. Actually, *I'm* keeping *you*."

"I'm not the right man for you. You deserve someone who doesn't bring the shit I do."

"I'm not innocent, either. You know this firsthand. You seem to get off on that side of me."

"There's no turning back once you take this step. Do you understand this? No changing your mind. No escape."

"You don't frighten me."

"Think carefully about what you are committing to. I will own all of you. Body, mind, and soul."

"I find that acceptable since you own my heart."

Fuck.

I dropped my forehead against hers. "I'm trying to do the right thing. Why won't you let me do the right thing?"

"Because everyone's version of the right thing was never my style." She paused, took a deep breath, and then continued. "I have a proposition for you."

Lifting my head, I stared into her onyx eyes.

"If you can actually see me living a life with someone else, marrying someone else, having a family with someone else, I'll walk away." My fingers flexed on her wrists. "But if you love me the way I believe you do, then you put aside this stupid sense of chivalry, take me to Vegas, and marry me tonight."

"You want to elope?"

"Do you love me, Simon?"

"You already know how I feel."

"Do I? All I've heard so far are parts of a well-known quote."

I cupped her face and then ran a thumb over her lips and down her throat.

"I love you, Olympia Nyx Mykos."

"Was that so hard?"

"You've sealed your fate. I hope you understand this."

"As that quote you never finished goes: If you love someone, set them free. If they come back, they're yours. I'm yours, Simon."

"Are you serious about Vegas?"

"I'm always serious about Vegas."

"Then we have a flight to catch."

"What about the Drakos empire? Won't they miss you?"

"I'll just tell them the goddess of night captured my soul."

"I really am a bad influence on you. There may be hope of corrupting you yet."

"Proposition accepted."

I smiled down at her, knowing life with her would never be boring.

Want to see how Penny and Hagen got their start?
Read Master of Sin
Or
Start a brand new series in the underworld of New York City
with Dangerous King

The End

MASTER OF SIN - GODS OF VEGAS
BOOK 1

Read the first book in the Gods of Vegas Series:

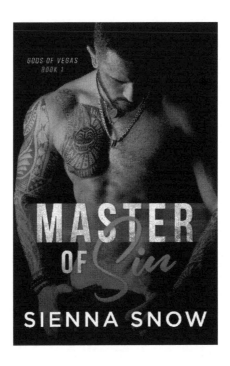

https://geni.us/MasterOfSin

It was always him...

The one I shouldn't want, shouldn't crave, the one who could destroy my carefully built life.

Hagen Lykaios was the essence of sin, indulgence, and danger - everything I knew to avoid.

All it took was one unexpected touch, and he consumed me, left me begging, needy, and hungry for more.

He said if I entered his world he would corrupt me, own me, and change all that I had ever known...and you know what? *I went anyway.*

BOOKS BY SIENNA

Rules of Engagement

Rule Breaker

Rule Master

Rule Changer

Politics of Love

Celebrity

Senator

Commander

Gods of Vegas

Master of Sin

Master of Games

Master of Revenge

Master of Secrets

Master of Control

Master of Fortune

Sweetest Sin

Intrigued By Love

Street Kings

Dangerous King

Vicious Prince

Deceptive Knight

Ruthless Heir (Feb 2023)

Standalones

Reckless Romeo (A Cocky Hero Club Novel)

Dirty Arrangement (A Blurred Lines Collective) - (Oct - 2022)

Collections

Take Me To Bed (Limited Run Anthology - 2019)

Meet Me Under The Mistletoe (Limited Run Anthology - 2021)

Darkly Ever After (An Organized Crime Anthology) (May 2022)

Happily Ever after Cookbook (Recipes from your favorite authors)

Nightingale (A charity anthology in support of Ukraine) - (April 2022)

ABOUT THE AUTHOR

Inspired by her years working in corporate America, Sienna loves to serve up stories woven around confident and successful women who know what they want and how to get it, both in – and out – of the bedroom.

Her heroines are fresh, well-educated, and often find love and romance through atypical circumstances. Sienna treats her readers to enticing slices of hot romance infused with empowerment and indulgent satisfaction.

Sienna loves the life of travel and adventure. She plans to visit even the farthest corners of the world and delight in experiencing the variety of cultures along the way. When she isn't writing or traveling, Sienna is working on her "happily ever after" with her husband and children.

Sign up for her newsletter for notification of releases, book sales, events and so much more.
http://www.siennasnow.com/newsletter
contact@siennasnow.com

facebook.com/authorsiennasnow

twitter.com/sienna_snow

instagram.com/bysiennasnow

tiktok.com/@authorsiennasnow

Made in the USA
Columbia, SC
01 April 2022

58370970R00146